The Clay Writer

Zoran Živković

The Clay Writer

Shaping in Creative Writing

 Springer

Zoran Živković
Novi Beograd, Serbia

ISBN 978-3-030-19752-0   ISBN 978-3-030-19753-7   (eBook)
https://doi.org/10.1007/978-3-030-19753-7

This Springer imprint is published by the registered company Springer Nature Switzerland AG
The registered company address is: Gewerbestrasse 11, 6330 Cham, Switzerland

To Ivana

Preface

The first seventy years of my life were very bookish indeed.

My first encounter with books occurred when I was only three years old. My mother used to read to me almost every evening; I couldn't fall asleep without hearing at least a few pages. Luckily, that was well before the glorious days of the Internet era with its surrogate mothers in the shape of a variety of digital gadgets that do anything but inspire their users to love reading, love literature and love books.

I started reading books myself at the age of eight and haven't stopped since. I studied comparative literature; both my MA and Ph.D. theses were about literary subjects. Then, I commenced translating, mostly from English; my translator's opus contains more than seventy books. The next step was publishing books; first as an editor and then as an independent publisher, I produced about three hundred editions.

I quit that job in order to become an author. In three decades, I have written thirty books—twenty-two fiction and eight non-fiction. They were brought out in nearly two hundred editions in twenty-five countries around the world, including my native Serbia.

Eventually, I embarked on my final bookish voyage. Relying on my long experience in the world of books, I began instructing others on how to write fiction. I spent the last ten years before my retirement in 2017 as a Professor at the Faculty of Philology, University of Belgrade, teaching creative writing. During that decade I was a mentor to more than four hundred students who wrote on average seven short stories each—amounting to nearly three thousand pieces of fiction.

I wish I could say I was at least partly as fruitful in my last literary endeavour as I was (hopefully) in the previous ones, but it is far from certain. The fruitfulness depends on the yardstick one uses to measure it. If the objective of my creative writing course was to create writers, then it might seem a total failure. As far as I know, so far only a couple of my students have managed to make their modest literary debut after having worked with me: namely their first book appeared.

But maybe I should slightly change the yardstick without changing the main objective of my creative writing course: to create writers. Maybe it is still possible to achieve this goal—it only requires more time. In early 2019, as I write this Preface, it is only a decade since I got started with the first generation of my students. Ten years is simply not long enough for them to have become writers. After all, it was I myself who used to tell them, in the very first class, that one does not become a writer before the age of fifty.

If what seemed to my students a rather discouraging estimate happens to be correct, I can hardly expect to be still around in twenty years to verify how successful I was as a creative writing professor. But I have grounds to hope that at least some of the prose seeds I planted will eventually grow into literary trees. As a mentor, I believe I gave them the best I could—the best any mentor is able to: the initial impetus. The rest is up to them.

Their lives would not have to be as bookish as mine. In order to become a good writer, it is by no means necessary to follow in my footsteps all the way—to be a translator, an editor, a publisher, a literary scholar… There is only one fundamental requirement: to read unceasingly and insatiably. It is principally through reading that a writer is shaped.

Unfortunately, the vast majority of my students are the contemporaries of the Internet era. They are incomparably more skilful than my humble self when it comes to handling various digital gadgets, but reading is hardly their favourite activity. Those rare few among them who were fortunate enough to listen to their mother's reading in the evening instead of solitarily playing with an iPhone or a tablet are most likely to become the highest literary trees.

I wish so much I had the chance to read their books when their time eventually comes. I would be in my early nineties then. Who knows, maybe they are not entirely unattainable after all…

Novi Beograd, Serbia   Zoran Živković
March 2019

Contents

Part I
Essays

1

The Clay Writer

1.1 Introduction

From 2007 until my retirement at the end of 2017, I taught two courses in the creative writing of literary prose at the Faculty of Philology, University of Belgrade. The first and principal one was intended for regularly matriculating students; the second—the summer school of creative writing—for non-academic participants. I always started both courses by offering four reasons why those attending them should not be there.

In terms of the students, this approach was justified even from a practical point of view. As a rule, more than fifty of them would appear at the first class, which significantly surpassed the number of participants I hoped for (twenty or so), lest the quality of the course should suffer. This discouraging introduction, however, seemed quite inappropriate for the summer school attendees since (as opposed to the students, who had other elective

© Springer Nature Switzerland AG 2019
Z. Živković, *The Clay Writer*,
https://doi.org/10.1007/978-3-030-19753-7_1

courses available if they did not enroll on the creative writing course) they had actually paid in order to participate in that very course of mine. Discouraging them from creative writing seemed cynical. As if I were telling them: "You just threw your money away."

In spite of this inappropriateness, I still did not refrain from giving them the four reasons. I considered it my supreme obligation toward both the students and the summer school attendees. A few participants from both groups—especially the latter—applied for the creative writing course more or less convinced that here they would learn, if not everything, then at least the essential points of what it takes to become a writer. I learned this from a small survey I conducted when I was getting to know them, before I explained the sobering reasons.

Once I had done so, not a single one of the participants amongst either the students or the summer school attendees left the course, although my reasons seemed to me to be quite convincing. The students remained because they mostly came to class without any great expectation of becoming writers, so they weren't overly disappointed by my announcing that my course would not lead to this result. In fact, they generally came without any expectation at all. They were enticed most often by curiosity, the fact that creative writing is in fashion as a relatively new academic subject in Serbia, as well as by rumors encountered on internet forums that I am not usually a strict teacher. Namely, it was no secret that giving low grades to my students was not my practice. I would tell them myself, soon after the beginning of the course, that I would not fail them. I was proud of the fact that I managed to teach all those who remained on the course to produce, after two semesters, a prose text of at least the lowest grade, no matter how unlikely that might seem after their first attempts, in the early stages of my course, before I had begun training them.

(The reduction of the large initial number of students to the desired twenty-odd eventually came about for more prosaic reasons. Most of those who dropped the course did so as soon as they found out that they were to write seven stories during the academic year—prose texts amounting to some forty thousand characters with spaces. Apparently, they had hoped that the course would be "theoretical," that they would become trained writers not by writing anything, but just by learning the theory of writing prose. Likewise, a significant number left the course after I informed them that class attendance was obligatory, that they had the right to only two unjustified absences during the semester.)

In the summer school, everyone remained, of course, primarily because they had paid to attend. So that they wouldn't be too disappointed, as soon as I informed them of the aggravating reasons, I would rush to offer them the mitigating ones. I indicated to them, in fact, why my course in creative writing, while not making them into writers, would still be useful on the road to perhaps becoming writers some day—that, in fact, the money they had invested had not been wasted. The latter reasons were no less convincing than the former ones. Not once did I receive a "complaint" when we parted after our one or two month-long literary gatherings. On the contrary, most of the summer school participants were interested in continuing to receive my mentoring in creative writing even after the end of the summer course.

It was mostly for the students that I primarily formulated the reasons for mediating their expectations that the creative writing course would turn them into writers. Still, they also applied to the non-academic participants, even though their demographics were quite varied in terms of age, education, reading history and writing experience, so that naturally there were exceptions to whom certain reasons did not apply, or at least only in part.

So, finally, here are the four reasons that were intended to discourage participants from taking my course in creative writing or, in a broader sense, from writing at all.

1. *Even the highest grade at the end of the creative writing course did not mean that the participant had become a writer. One does not become a prose writer before the age of fifty.*

As statistics show, in every field of creativity there is an age when one achieves the most. In mathematics, for instance, that peak falls in the late twenties. In physics, in the early thirties. In the arts, maturity is reached earliest in music. The appearance of a *wunderkind* is still not uncommon there. However, in prose, there have not been genius children or young people for a long time—if there ever were any at all. There are very few writers, at least in the literature of the twentieth century, who wrote their best work before they turned fifty. (A famous exception in the nineteenth century was Anton Pavlovich Chekhov, who wrote the main part of his remarkable body of work in his twenties and thirties, while he didn't write at all in his fifties because he died at the age of forty-four.)

I reckoned that this would discourage students from the early twenty-first century. They are, namely, members of the so-called "instant generation," whose ideal, regardless of what they do, is to become successful as soon as possible, preferably overnight. Fame is best reached via shortcuts. Their ambitions suddenly deflate if they have to invest literally decades of effort in achieving success, without any guarantee that it will happen at all, as is the case with literary prose.

In order to mock this of thinking, I suggested that—if they really cared about instant success at any cost—they search for it in some other field of creativity where achievements can be reached at a much younger age, and with a lot less investment of effort, than in literature. That would first be in popular folk music. It is enough if one is quite humbly gifted with a voice and good looks, and starts singing on one of the popular television shows for young talents. Sports are also an area where one achieves success in one's youth. The only problem is that here talent is not enough—for serious achievements, long and strenuous training is demanded.

2. *In order to become a writer, it is necessary first to read a lot.*

We have been writing literature for almost two and a half thousand years. Over that long period, a truly voluminous corpus of prose works has been created. No matter how long we live, it wouldn't be nearly enough, even if we did nothing else but read, to embrace everything that has ever been written. Fortunately, it is also not necessary. It has long since been known that 95% of most stuff is worthless. Prose is no exception in this regard. As with everything else, there are many more sloppy creations than valuable ones. Still, whatever is left after we throw out the slop is still quite voluminous. Even if we further narrowed the circle of quality so that we chose not only the best, but the best of the best, it would take decades to read it all. Our civilization suffers from scribomania, so even only one permil of what is written—let's say that only such a tiny percentage belongs to the best of the best—barely fits into the span of a human life. Soon, however, if this ever-growing scribomania continues, an entire human lifespan will no longer be enough to master the *crème de la crème* of world literature.

That is why there are no writers before the age of fifty. The preparatory work simply demands a lot of time. There are no shortcuts here. Talent is received at birth, while reading experience is obtained through long-lasting dedication. There are artistic disciplines in which talent is enough, but prose writing does not fall among them. In that, talent without reading experience is not enough.

If one doesn't read what truly is the best of world literature, then one simply cannot expect to become a good writer. Primarily because familiarity with our literary heritage is the most fertile ground for planting new seedlings of prose. There is not a better, more complete, and more useful course in the creative writing of literary prose than that of the creative reading of literary prose. Everything you ever wanted to know about the secrets of creating literary prose is contained in a heritage comprising the highest quality literary models. Excellent teachers await you there, both female and male, unmatched among those who nowadays professionally teach creative writing.

Reading the best literary works is also obligatory because a writer without enough reading experience might believe that they have come up with something original, when it was already discovered long ago. They would be breaking ice that has long since been penetrated. There is a famous anecdote about a professor who, in the following way, evaluated a story by one of his students who proclaimed that the less he read, the better he would write: "Your story is good and original. The problem, however, is that where it is good it is not original, and where it is original, it is not good."

There is also an "ethical" reason which demands that, before we ourselves start writing prose, we read the works of the great masters before us. If we don't do so, do we have the right to expect that our works will be read by those who come after? For writers, reading is, along with other things, also a kind of payment of a debt before incurring it.

Unfortunately, reading is decidedly not a favorite pastime of the "instant generation," even among students of literature. Even they, at least from time to time, rely on the shortcuts which flood the internet. There is practically no great literary work that has not been made into a movie, and ultimately there are summaries or significantly abbreviated versions. Such alternatives to reading can occasionally be useful to students before exams where their overall knowledge is tested, but they are completely useless in a creative writing course. Here, it is unmistakably evident whether a student has read the work in its original form. I hoped that this unavoidable imperative of truly wide-ranging reading would be sure to discourage students who have no inclination toward it, and most of them do not.

3. *In Serbia, there has never yet been a writer who earned their living solely from writing literary prose, and the probability is high that there never will be.*

Students choose an elective course, among other things, according to whether it will be of use to them in their further professional lives. If a student applies for a course in creative writing, it is only natural to suppose that they hope to be able one day to support themselves by means of their literary work. In order for such hopes not to be inappropriately high, it is important to make students aware of the unfortunate situation on the domestic literary scene.

In Serbia at the end of the second decade of the twenty-first century, one simply cannot expect to be a professional writer. To live, even humbly, just from writing, it is necessary that the number of books sold be significantly higher than a mere five hundred copies, which is the average print-run nowadays in this part of the world.

It simply cannot be better in a country with a relatively modest population of slightly over seven million, where—according to official statistics—nearly 20% of the inhabitants are only partially literate, while another 60% or so, while being technically literate, do not read a single book in a year (and never think of buying one), and are even generally proud of that fact. (Here it is not of much comfort that the situation is similar in most other countries, even in those which are considered to be the most highly cultivated...) The annual Belgrade Book Fair, the largest book exhibition in the country, is the best indicator of the pitiful state of things. The number of visitors has never risen above 250,000, and that is just 3% of the population.

Anyone who intends to become a writer should reconcile themselves to the fact that it will not be their main occupation. They will have to pay the bills in some other way, while writing won't be much more than a hobby. When I relate this sad situation to the students, there is always someone who turns my attention to the fact that everything is not quite as gloomy as I depict it. Even here, namely, there are writers whose books sell in high print runs.

Indeed there are, and I haven't overlooked them. If nothing else, even had I wanted to, I certainly could not have overlooked the billboards decorating the paths to the exhibition halls at the Book Fair—billboards which, in an unnaturally large format, show the smiling faces of authoresses and authors excited by the high volume sales of their books. I remind the student who doubted my memory, then, of the thing *they* have overlooked—the precise title of my course: the creative writing of *literary* prose.

The troubles described await you if you decide to work on *literary* prose. For in addition to that, there is also *entertaining*, or *popular* prose. If one works on that, then writing really can be one's main occupation. There, high print runs truly do get published, and there are also other positive aspects. In order to write popular prose, you need practically no preparatory work. You don't have to dedicate yourself in the least to reading a lot, nor do you need a course in creative writing. Chiefly, you need some basic literacy, and often not even that much.

The situation is fairly similar to that in music. The largest concert halls for classical music have about four thousand seats, which is negligible when compared to the open spaces where the greats of popular music perform in front of hundreds of thousands of fans who are interested only in mindless entertainment, not caring at all if the singer has a trained voice or is just screaming.

Although I don't tell the students this, so as not to endanger my main intention of lowering the number of course participants, the division here is not black-and-white. Of course it is not necessarily true that literary prose is low volume and unpopular. On the contrary, it can certainly be successful in this aspect as well. The field of its effect must be widened beyond the linguistic milieu in which it was created. When books of literary prose begin to appear in translation in other countries, their overall print runs can exceed those reached by popular authors, which are almost always limited to their language of origin. And in order for that to happen, it is necessary, above all, to fulfil one condition—to write a genuinely good work of literary prose.

4. *I cannot make anyone into a writer.*

This is my crowning reason. The previous three can be insufficient if the participant has truly decided to attend the course in writing literary prose at any cost, regardless of the barriers standing in their way, but my open admission that I am not a wizard and that I cannot do anything for them, must by necessity turn them off. Truly, I cannot make anyone into a writer.

Here, however, one small supplemental factor ensues which offers a certain escape from the seemingly inevitable conclusion that a course in writing literary prose is meaningless. I cannot make anyone into a writer—unless that person is already that, at least in an embryonic state. Unless they have the slightest talent for prose.

The analogy with the talent for singing will help to explain this better. Let us imagine that someone really wants to turn my humble self into an opera singer. For that purpose, they could hire the best singing teacher available. Unfortunately, no matter how hard the teacher tries, it will all be in vain. Although I am not tone-deaf, I simply don't have a singing voice. I will never be an opera singer.

However, if I did have a singing voice—even a tiny one—then the voice coach's efforts would pay off. Well, perhaps I would never reach the Metropolitan or La Scala, but nor would I hesitate to start singing in public, unlike at present, when even the thought of doing so terrifies me. The teacher would certainly help me hone my raw talent, which only suffices for very amateurish singing.

The same is true of prose. There is no mentor in literary prose-writing who can help a writer-to-be who is completely lacking in literary talent. It is a hopeless case. If, however, a certain talent does exist, no matter how humble, then work with a mentor can certainly be useful. If their labour ultimately does not bring in a Nobel Prize for Literature, it could at least help train the writer to shape their prose well enough that they can confidently submit it for publication. And is that a small achievement for a course in writing literary prose?

Two questions are asked in relation to the foregoing.

The first is: how does one establish the existence, or rather non-existence, of literary talent? With a singing voice it is easy. It is unnecessary for the person being tested to sing an entire aria. It's practically enough for them to open their mouth. Even those for whom singing is not a profession will be able effortlessly to offer a diagnosis in just a few seconds. With prose, perhaps it will not be as simple when laypeople evaluate whether a writer is talented or not, but a creative writing mentor, or a professor of literature, will certainly not have to read a large quantity of text to determine that. A page will be enough, sometimes even just a paragraph. The professional and trained eye sees everything there immediately.

When I receive the first stories of the participants in my creative writing course, written immediately after the introductory class, before any instruction from me, I easily determine whether a prose voice can be heard in them or not. Those who don't have it, however, I never tell. This is not just out of respect toward would-be-writers who are, by the nature of things, quite sensitive, something about which I am painstaking during the entire course. No one in my classes has ever felt insulted, no matter if what they have written merits harsh judgment or even ridicule. I avoid offering my diagnosis not because I am unsure of it, since I have never once been mistaken in my first evaluation. I keep it to myself, taught by one of my own experiences long ago.

One written assignment I composed at the end of elementary school must have given my literature teacher every reason to grab her head and practically cry out, "Anything might happen to you, Živković, but one thing is clear—you'll never become a writer." A prose voice can possibly not be heard because it really is not there, which is the most common case, but also because it is hidden and will only appear, perhaps, somewhat later.

The other question is of essential importance: how can a mentor in the writing of literary prose in any way help students with a certain literary talent, and also, what is the best way to do so? A discussion has been ongoing among professionals about these key questions for the

130 years or so which have passed since the founding of the first academic programs that could be defined as embryonic creative writing courses in the modern sense. These discussions, it seems, are still far from reaching a more or less general agreement, although that does not stop the teaching of creative writing courses all over the world, now more than ever. This book is an attempt to offer a humble contribution to shedding light on the central problem of the academic subject of the writing of literary prose, from the perspective of many years of teaching experience.

1.2   The Definition of Creative Writing

Despite its ubiquity, the term creative writing remains ambiguous. This strikes me afresh at the start of every course in literary prose-writing when I ask newly enrolled students what their expectations are. The answers I get are quite various. Most numerous are the students who expect nothing. If they have any idea about creative writing, it is vague at best. They have decided to check it out simply because this subject is fashionable, or out of pure curiosity.

Of those who do expect something, some think of creative writing as a theoretical course where one can learn, in summary form, about the basics of literature, which might aid them in keeping up with other courses. Others see creative writing as an historical course where an overview is presented of the various poetics and their demands upon writers from ancient times until our own day. Finally, there is a third group who have tried their hand at writing to a greater or lesser extent. They hope that creative writing will help them improve their writing skills, although they have no idea of how the course might look (unless, of course, they have informed themselves by asking older colleagues who have already taken it).[1]

Once I have presented the details of the course to students, as well as what is expected from them, a certain number inevitably withdraw. Whatever I failed to achieve with my introduction elaborating the four convincing reasons to drop the course, I do finally manage by confronting them with the obligations it entails. Those obligations mostly deter the students who thought the course to be theoretical or historical, then to a somewhat smaller extent those who just happened upon it, while they are least problematic to those with a certain amount of writing experience.

When the classroom holds only those students who have resolved, despite all the barriers, to attend my course, I ask them quite a confusing question: what the exact name of it is? Most often I get the answer which seems to be obvious—"creative writing". Only rare students cite the full name: "The creative writing of literary prose".

Without this additional determiner, however, the very term "creative writing" is not complete and does not necessarily imply literary prose, or even prose at all. That's the way it has been since the mid-1920s, when this syntagma was first introduced in the sense of the teaching of writing. At that time, it referred to prose, poetry, and drama. At the end of the second decade of the twenty-first century, creative writing is related to an entire spectrum of fields which are connected only by the fact that they appear in written form.

---

[1]Among the non-academic attendees of the course in summer school, this third kind of expectation about creative writing was most common. Almost all the participants have some sort of writing experience, and they enroll in the course hoping that they will learn something new about prose writing.

At universities, creative writing is still primarily related to the three basic literary genres—prose, poetry, and drama—but now, especially in the USA, those have been expanded. Not only are special courses established for the individual types of genre (stories, novellas, novels, film and television scripts) but also for other, extra-literary genres (essays, academic writing, journalism…).

The offer of creative writing courses outside the university is much more miscellaneous. So, for example, the *Gotham Writers' Workshop* in New York,[2] one of the leading contemporary extra-academic institutions that deals with creative writing, has literally scores of special courses[3]: action: article writing, blog basics, blog writing, business writing, character development, children's book writing, comics and graphic novels, creative nonfiction 101, creative writing 101, dialogue writing, essay and opinion writing, fiction writing, food writing, grammar!, hit send: publishing short nonfiction, how to get published, humor writing, in(verse): poetic techniques for non-poets, just write, memoir writing, mystery writing, nonfiction book proposal, novel writing, pen on fire, personal essay writing, poetry writing, reading fiction, romance writing, science fiction and fantasy writing, scriptwriting, songwriting, stand-up comedy writing, teen scriptwriting, travel writing, true story: teen creative nonfiction, unbound: teen creative writing, video game writing…

In spite of a certain amount of course overlap, there is obviously a large variety of aspects of creative writing. Therefore it is simply not enough to use just this basic term without a narrower definition. Taken only in itself,

---

[2]*Gotham Writers' Workshop* (http://www.writingclasses.com/—last accessed March 19th, 2019).

[3]This offering was true at the end of 2018. The programs change often according to what kind of writing is most sought for on the market.

creative writing is so variegated and so vague a concept that if you Google it in English, you get an incredible result of more than 300 million entries (at the end of 2018). Even if you do it for a smaller language like Serbian, you get more than 150,000 entries. Just a quick overview of those entries proves that the term is used with a huge range of meanings, which are often rather unrelated.

The original sin which led to this vagueness rests on the soul of William Hughes Mearns, an American dramatist and novelist, respected in his time primarily for his insistence on the teaching of prose writing. In his book *Creative Youth*,[4] published in 1925, Mearns first used the syntagma "creative writing" to indicate a subject that was being taught in junior high schools. Although courses in prose and poetry writing were introduced at the college level in the USA in the mid-1880s, they previously had no common name. Soon after 1925 creative writing became a generally accepted term in the nomenclature of junior high subjects. At first, it was thought generally clear what the term meant, but in time it became more and more necessary to use it with additional determiners.

Mearns did not invent this syntagma. He borrowed it from Ralph Waldo Emerson, the American writer, lecturer, and essayist. In a lecture entitled "The American Scholar," delivered on August 21, 1837 at the Phi Beta Kappa fraternity in Cambridge, Massachusetts, Emerson pronounced—as it would later turn out—the far-reaching sentence, "There is then creative reading as well as creative writing."[5]

---

[4]William Hughes Mearns, *Creative Youth: How a School Environment Set Free the Creative Spirit*.
[5]Ralph Waldo Emerson, "The American Scholar." In *Selected Writings*, p. 51.

Under this concept, Emerson did not imply what we would today consider creative writing to be even in its broadest possible sense. In his lecture, he attacked the false erudition dominating American academic circles of the time, especially among literary scholars. He confronted the gleaning of useless "knowledge" with the creative principle, from the use of language, through the approach to reading, to writing itself.

The attempt, in our time, to define the basic concept of "creative writing" requires the clarification of both parts of the syntagma. As far as "writing" goes, there is generally no lack of clarity. Without an additional determiner, it can be—as we saw in the example of the "Gotham Writers' Workshop"—almost anything expressed in written form. The main ambiguity is related to the first part of the phrase, "creative."

Already from the fact that we call something "creative writing," it follows that it would be in opposition to something we might call "uncreative writing." What would the difference be between these two writing forms?

Slovene writer and Professor of Creative Writing, Andrej Blatnik, approached the problem of separating creative from uncreative writing at the beginning of his book *Short Story Writing: from First Draft to Publication.*

"Writing short stories is indeed *creative* writing. Such writing differs from *functional* in the fact that it moves away from genre forms. If someone still sends postcards from the seaside, and writes on them 'Wish you were here' and signs it, they have fulfilled the genre's model. The message is that they are where they are supposed to be. If they add their impressions of the air and water temperatures, they add something of cognitive content to the model—the message is what it is like there. With adjectives ('the water is *very warm*'), they are perhaps increasing the value of the message, but they still have not stepped away from the model. Even a postcard from the seaside can be creative in addition to informative, it can contain valorization and esthetic dimensions by encompassing the corresponding knowledge in the corresponding elevated or 'low-brow' language ('you just wouldn't believe how they've jacked up the price of beer here'), and with those dimensions raise the threshold for entering the text, because with a less general way of expression—let's say by using dialect or slang—the number decreases of those who can understand the meaning. It can be truly creative and end up in the collected works of famous authors or in an anthology of the most unusual postcards from the seaside (yes, such anthologies do exist). It is hard to imagine that a postcard saying just 'Wish you were here' would end up in an anthology, even if it were written by some noteworthy person. It is not creative enough, it creates nothing that would make it stand out from the model of a practically infinite number of the same kind."[6]

Although his terminological use is imprecise, Professor Blatnik correctly points out the essential difference between "uncreative" and "creative" writing. The first, which the Slovene author describes as "genre form," "functional," that which comes about according to "a form," "a model," "a general way of expression"—is in fact *non-artistic*, while the other, which is defined as "esthetic" and contains "value dimensions" and "corresponding knowledge" expressed in differing language registers—is *artistic*.

A postcard from the seaside will also fall into the category of "creative writing" if what is written on it has a certain amount of artistic value. It makes no difference,

[6]Andrej Blatnik, *Pisanje kratke zgodbe: Od prvopisa do natisa*. The quote is according to the first Croatian version: Andrej Blatnik (2010), *Pisanje kratke priče: od prvopisa do tiska*, Zagreb, CeKaPe.

actually, whether it is a postcard or any other piece of paper on which something is written. The postcard is taken only as an example of a place for writing which is exceptionally rarely used for articulating an artistic text. In principle, the same is also true of a normal piece of paper on which, up until the computer age, artistic texts most often appeared. The percentage of non-artistic texts on pieces of paper corresponds to the percentage of banal postcards. This is in the nature of things. Artistic texts—both on normal pieces of paper and on postcards, or even on any other surface used for writing—are significantly rarer than non-artistic ones.

If he had wished to use a more modern example than a postcard, Professor Blatnik could have chosen the SMS message. By far the highest number of these short texts exchanged via cellphone have no artistic value at all. Yet, similarly to the anthology of artistically composed postcards, recently the first artistic SMS works have appeared.

Differentiating "uncreative" from "creative" writing as the *non-artistic* from the *artistic* is suitable only when a literary text is in question. It is already in principle inapplicable to most of the courses of the Gotham Writers' Workshop. What, if anything, can be artistic in the writing of sketches, for example, or of business letters, non-literary works, or even about food? All courses of this sort fall into the category of *non-artistic*. Here, in fact, it makes no sense whatsoever to talk about "uncreative" and "creative." Ultimately, one could speak of "unskillful" or "skillful." The problem is probably that "creative" seems to be more serious and of higher quality for the prefix of a course than "skillful."

Meanwhile, even those courses that formally belong to the field of literature do not necessarily include artistic ambitions. It is quite possible that, for example, a course on novel writing pays much more attention to market value than artistic value. No one at Gotham has a prejudice against prose which is mainly written for a market, no matter how artistically worthless it is, if it makes a better profit than artistic prose.[7]

The conditions are better in the framework of academic programs for creative prose writing. In such courses, artistic quality usually outweighs market quality. Generally speaking, the division between the two value systems is less strict at universities in the USA than at European ones, where the market potential of a literary work is still not a justification for it being artistically worthless.

When I was defining the title of my course, I had to take two differentiations into consideration: *generic* and *axiological.* First of all, it was necessary, along with the basic concept, "creative writing," to add the defining "prose" in order to indicate that it is not one of the non-artistic courses in creative writing (like those offered, for example, at Gotham) but one that is related to one of the three basic literary genres. The adjective "literary (i.e. artistic)" is there in order to differentiate it from the artistically worthless, *popular.* (Some courses in creative writing, namely, could easily be called the "creative writing of popular prose.")

If I had had *carte blanche* in choosing the name of the course I teach—but I did not, because the phrase "creative writing" has long since been established as the basic name of this type of academic subject—I certainly would have removed "creative" as being a pleonasm. The "writing of literary prose" would be enough by itself. What else could

---

[7]That which is "artistic" is not, of course, precluded from being "marketable," but that is the exception rather than the rule. Popular literature, that which does well on the market, is only rarely artistically valuable. One might say it is just the nature of things.

it be than creative? The writing of literary prose lies at the very peak of artistic creation.

For those who are interested in the creative writing of popular prose—and such authors are not small in number where the market value of literature holds a privileged place—no course, in fact, is even necessary. There is a shortcut to the desired goal—writing works which will have a high market value. There are computer programs for sale which will do most of the work of the "writer."[8]

The "author" whose name will end up on the cover is only required to enter the outline of the forthcoming work. The program will then ask them a series of questions. If they choose to "write" a novel, it will ask them first what genre they want it to belong to, which of the offered topics they choose, which sort of plot they prefer, how many female and how many male characters they want, what features are to embellish the protagonist, whether the work should have lots of scenes of sex and violence or whether it should be moderate in that sense, whether dialogue has precedence over description, action over contemplation—and so on, down to the last detail.

Once the propositions are given, the "writer" just has to wait for their printer to produce a completely finished product: a novel "written" according to their demands and signed with their name. The computer program composes a collage of the parts it has ready prepared in a large memory bank. The segments are relatively skillfully connected, so the untrained eye will not notice the seams between them. From a technical standpoint, the manuscript has the form of a novel, and the text is at least meaningfully

---

[8]In addition to computer writing programs there is another shortcut for "writers" who are not averse to this sort of "cooperation." One can also use a ghostwriter.

composed in an elementary way, which is actually the minimum expected of popular prose.

The "author" just has to hope that they have chosen the right combination of elements offered and have "written" a work that will be appealing first to a literary agent, then to a publisher, and finally to readers of light, entertaining literature. If they really get lucky, the novel might become a bestseller, and that is the highpoint in the marketing system of values.

Such a shortcut is impossible when we speak of literary prose. As opposed to popular literature which can be reduced to models, patterns, and forms so that it can be easily translated into digital language, literary prose is unique in all important senses, impossible to capture by any sort of algorithm. Computers are unable to "create" it. Only the human brain can write it—and not just any brain, but the mind of an artist.[9]

---

[9]Though unwillingly, I must dilute what I have just written about computers. When I say that they are unable to create artistic prose, I have the current state of computer technology in mind. The situation in that field, however, is changing quite rapidly, and I already "got burned" once because I was not farseeing enough. In 1999, when I wrote the novel *The Book*, it seemed to me that the CD-ROM would be the last word in computer advancement, and so I finished the book with the triumph of this digital miracle over Gutenberg's invention. Yet, just ten years later CD-ROMs had become obsolete. It would be much more suitable for the victor over books on paper to be some sort of digital reader, but who could predict, in the penultimate year of the twentieth century that such readers would appear so quickly? (Some of my foreign publishers who want to put out *The Book* persistently propose that I rewrite the end of the novel so that the CD-ROM is exchanged for a digital reader. However, I refuse with equal persistence. Such interventions could turn into a "never-ending story." What will happen if the digital reader heads into oblivion in the next ten years? Should I keep forever adapting the end of the novel according to the development of computer technology?) In terms of artistic ability, it seems to me that it will remain out of reach to computers no matter how much they improve in a linear fashion. Still, the situation could change if a fundamental advancement occurs. Who knows, perhaps the rumoured quantum computers will be able to cope with artistic creation. If that happens, then we will have to change our point of view from the foundations up, not only about creative writing, but regarding almost all human activities. The world that will come about then will differ greatly from the present one…

Such a circumstance opens up another important question. If literary prose cannot be encompassed by any sort of algorithm, how can one even teach how it is written? What would be the curriculum of the subject called the creative writing of literary prose? The answer is that actually there is no generally accepted curriculum, in spite of the fact that creative writing has been taught for more than 130 years.

And it is taught by two kinds of lecturers: experts in creative writing who have no writing experience whatsoever, and writers who have a formal education in literature (more rarely), or who do not (more commonly). Although, in the absence of a common curriculum, their programs are fairly varied, the main difference between the mentors is visible in the ultimate product of their courses. The experts in creative writing who are not writers produce new experts in creative writing who are also not writers. Writers, on the other hand, do not produce new writers. The best they can hope for is that the participants write better at the end of the course than they did at the beginning.

1.3   Writers as Mentors of Creative Writing

There are two essential questions which still raise ambiguity when talking about creative writing, even though the academic history of this subject already spans more than 130 years. First—what is the point of creative writing, that is, what does one hope to achieve with it? This question is usually asked in quite a simplified form: can creative writing create a writer? Second—who is the most suitable to teach creative writing?

I will deal with the first question in the final section of the Part I of this book, once I have presented my course in creative writing in detail. To the simplified version of this question, however, I can already give an answer now—likewise in simplified form. Creative writing cannot create a writer. Moreover, that should not be the purpose of a course in creative writing. Metaphorically speaking, the hurdle that should be jumped must be placed lower, at a height which can be overcome. A course or a program of creative writing makes sense even if those attending it are just better writers in the end than at the beginning. As to whether someone will become a writer, a whole series of circumstances have an influence, certainly not just whether they have attended a creative writing course or not. Even of those who are naturally talented enough not to need any mentorial assistance, not all will end up as writers.

As far as the second question goes, the answer is obvious at first glance. Who can better teach the writing of literary prose—to limit ourselves to this type—than those who write it themselves? Are those who have no writing experience more suitable than they, no matter how much they know about literature? The obviousness of this answer is opposed, however, by reality.

The largest number of creative writing lecturers at universities worldwide are not writers. This is especially true of the English-speaking world, which encompasses more than 95% of academic creative writing programs. There, such programs are run by experts with degrees in creative writing who quite rarely, if at all, are writers themselves. As a consequence, there is a betrayal of what should be the point of a creative writing program—that those who attend write better in the end. At such programs, new experts in creative writing are created, not better writers.

The advantage of a writer as a creative writing lecturer, as opposed to an expert in this field who does not write literature, is first of all practical in nature, and that is actually the kind of help most needed by someone learning to write. Both the writer and the creative writing expert without writing experience will easily notice what is not good in a text by a participant in the course or program, but only the writer will be able to offer them practical advice about improving it, that is, to teach them how a given problem is solved in prose writing. The only thing the participant can hope for from the creative writing expert who is not a writer is the general recommendation to fix what is not good. The practical value of this recommendation, however, is quite small. If the participant knew how to fix what was wrong, they would have written it properly in the first place.

At a small number of European universities where creative writing has been introduced, this subject is generally taught by writers. Among those who attend their classes some actually do become writers, and almost all of the participants write better at the end of the course.[10] This is not only in the technical, craftsmanship sense, though that is also indubitably important. Here one also gains insight into the essential aspects of creating prose. This can be expected only from the writer who has incorporated those aspects into their own prose works.

In that sense, there is a simple recommendation for those who intend to take a course in creative writing, but are hesitating about which to choose. They should be guided by the prose works of the writer holding the course. In them one unmistakably sees what they can expect from the course. The writer cannot teach

[10]Cerutti, Sofie (2011), *Creative Writing in Europe*, Utrecht, Kunstfactor.

something they do not know themselves. By the same logic, the creative writing lecturer who is not a writer can hardly teach something which will help you write better in a practical sense. And one must not forget, it is actually that—to write better—which is the goal of the course or program of creative writing.

However, not all writers—just because they are writers—are suitable to be creative writing lecturers. Most writers have never dealt with teaching this subject. That is usually because they have simply never had the opportunity. Still, even if they had, the question remains as to how many writers would decide to teach creative writing. For that undertaking, a certain understanding of the very creative act of writing is necessary in the first place, and only a few rare writers confront the fundamental question—how do they write?

Most writers—and the same is true, I imagine, of other artists as well—simply accept their own gift as something presupposed. They are visited by a mysterious inspiration about which there is no need to think whatsoever. Any attempt to fathom this puzzling state of the soul would only—they believe—dissolve the halo of mystery which means a lot to them because it seems to make them extraordinary, and besides, it would be fruitless, since inspiration, precisely because it is mysterious, cannot be translated into rational language.

And whatever is not translatable into the language of reason cannot be a subject taught academically. The only thing writers cloaked in the mystical cape of inspiration could offer to those who also want to become writers is the useless advice that they should somehow also obtain it—and then everything will be more or less all right. That would be the start and finish of their creative writing course.

That such an opinion truly does reign among writers is testified to by the book *How Writers Write*, which includes contributions by twenty-odd contemporary Serbian authors. I imagine that the composer of the anthology, Slaviša Lekić, wanted to use the title to get writers to speak out about the creative act itself. That is certainly a more challenging and interesting topic than, for example, the surroundings in which writing occurs, or the customs, rituals and habits of writers while they write, which the book's title could also imply. Most writers, however, actually wrote about that, even avoiding attempts at rationalizing the process of creating a work of fiction or poetry.

To be fair, the contributions about the writing environment are fairly interesting. To the careful reader, they remove a prejudice which also unjustifiably mystifies the creative act—the prejudice about there being a privileged writing environment. Every author in this anthology has a certain set of conditions which satisfy them while they are writing. There are even such authors who write every book under different circumstances. "When I wrote the short novel *Out of Control*," Vladan Matijević reports to us, "I was forced to walk frantically around the room from wall to wall, and to write standing up. [...] *R.C. Inevitable* I wrote at night. The stories from the book *Fairly Dead* I wrote lying down, mostly at night. *The Writer from Afar* I wrote by locking myself up in a country house, exhausting myself day and night."[11] The circumstances for writing are only as significant as the work which they produce is good. There are no generally accepted special

---

[11] *Kako pisci pišu [How Writers Write]*, p. 57.

circumstances for writing which will guarantee the creation of a good work.[12]

Of the writers who made contributions to *How Writers Write*, the following at least attempted to peer behind the mystical barrier of inspiration: David Albahari, Ljubica Arsić, Dragan Velikić, Nikola Vujčić, Mihajlo Pantić, Ljubomir Simović, and Vladimir Tasić. Here are some passages from their texts related to that topic.

David Albahari: "Most of my stories are hatched from the first sentences—those are sentences that come to me at unexpected moments. […] Except for the technical aspects of writing, all the rest—even after all these years—I see almost as a sort of mystical experience. I keep asking myself anew, who is actually dictating the text that pours from me, who gives shape to the story, and how does the story or novel know when it is finished? […] Probably it is necessary that something exists in a person—the thing usually called talent and which is gotten by unclear means—but all the rest is a matter of craftsmanship, the skill of emulation, and constant reading. Talent doesn't guarantee anything: without it there is no inspired writing, that is true, but correct, linguistically clean prose can be written by anyone who has enough feeling for and understanding of the use of language. Thus, writing can be learned, but such writing is not enough for that secretive transfer of real inspiration which, like all other mystical teachings, goes along just one path: from heart to heart."[13]

Ljubica Arsić: "…I reflect upon the new book that I need to write. The topic comes to me from nowhere, at least I think so; it visits me in that interval between

---

[12]In the beautiful humoresque "When I Started to Write," Jaroslav Hašek actually talks about the various conditions under which writers work.
[13]Op cit., pp. 12–13.

sleeping and waking when I surrender to the morning
or the rain tapping on the window. [...] It occupies me
like a passion, it acts on me like a spell that I have cast on
myself. [...] In certain special moments that don't depend
on me, I feel everything deeply hidden coming out and
gliding across the paper. Then writing is as easy as swim-
ming, it creates the illusion in me that it will always be so.
[...] I rarely correct what is written, merely a word here
or there that bothers me, looking for a better one. [...] I
grow sad when I finish writing a book. I feel that it is no
longer related to me in any way. That something, like in
the most intimate psychoanalysis, has emptied a glove that
now hangs loosely without a hand."[14]

Dragan Velikić: "I never have an outline, or even a story.
As I write, I am actually attempting to free myself [...] of
seemingly unimportant details which come in from the
boundaries of oblivion. They arrive unexpectedly, conjured
up by who-knows-what combination of words."[15]

Nikola Vujčić: "I write slowly and in spurts. Sometimes
months will even pass and I write nothing, but I think
'poetically,' I write out words, whole phrases, I 'grasp'
images that seem unusual to me and which could inspire a
poem or a poetic state. Thus, 'the poet' works in me daily.
[...] The preparations for the creation of a poem are a long
and mysterious process. Its appearance can be stimulated,
and this is most common, by a completely banal detail, a
word, an event, external and internal stimuli that imbue
each other. The inspiration (though I prefer to name
that as a special spiritual state) by which a poem comes
about in any case is a 'special state' of increased emotion

---

[14]Ibid., pp. 14, 16.
[15]Ibid., p. 25.

and sensitivity where the intensity of experiencing is enhanced."[16]

Mihajlo Pantić: "All my stories are autobiographical, but they have nothing to do with me. […] Everything is biography, even when I look at the wall, hear a bird singing beneath the window in the morning, or think about going to Canada, all of that, and everything else, enters the biography of my consciousness and can become the subject of a story, and it all has no special visible consequences for my life. […] I write stories when they want me to, when they appear to me, when they want to be told through me. […] Otherwise, I believe that the deepest urge to write is profoundly irrational. […] Sometimes, I get the impression that the story I'm writing already exists and that it is simply forcing me to transfer it into a state of being said, and sometimes I have a really murky idea about the direction in which I am supposed to head. Usually it is a particular detail, a character, a thought or a turnabout from which one should set off and let the words weave around it. […] Writing stories is exciting and fulfilling actually because of the fact that even the one who is writing does not know what they will tell him in the end. Writing stories is, likewise, generally speaking, movement in an unpredictable direction. […] As if the story itself, with its flow, its rising, its surfacing from language, imposes its own will on the writer who is forced to obey it. […] I write when I have a story in me, when it comes to me, I don't know from where, when I feel myself to be a voice that has to say something."[17]

Ljubomir Simović: "The creative process is not just writing. The time you spend at the desk, writing, is just one

---

[16]Ibid., pp. 38–40.
[17]Ibid., pp. 62, 64, 66–68.

part of the creative process. Writing, the author writes
down something that has been in preparation for a long
time, and which has gone through a lot of preceding
activities. Wherever they are, whatever they are doing,
the poet watches everything, listens to everything, takes
everything into consideration, everything is important to
them; they absorb everything because everything which
happens could be hiding the seed from which something
will sprout, or a spark that will set something ablaze and
cast light upon it. [...] To define and describe the creative process, usually the term inspiration is used. [...] It
does not appear like lightning. It is achieved through constant concentration, by a focus that is never interrupted,
not when you go to the store, not when you get on the
bus, not when you get off the train. [...] And what does it
mean to be inspired? It means to arrive in a state where the
invisible is seen, the unknown is known, and the unsaid is
spoken. In the most fortunate case, it means to go through
a door not there into a world that does not exist. It means
going into non-reality, which will become reality in a
poem or because of a poem."[18]

Vladimir Tasić: "The passage from wasting time to writing is not dramatic. There's no earthquake, no fireworks,
none of the music which accompanies the epiphany of the
apes in Kubrick's film. The rhythms of everyday life grad-
ually change. [...] The writer is always at work. The truth
about that work... I'm speaking for myself... is very simple: observe, eavesdrop, note down, if possible from the
shadows. All the rest is just posing for a calendar."[19]

I myself have a text in the anthology *How Writers Write*.
In it, I tried to shed light on the act of creating a work of

---

[18]Ibid., pp. 79–80.
[19]Ibid., pp. 82, 86.

prose, without referring to mystical inspiration, to make it as rational as humanly possible.

"I begin writing just after waking up, when an image or the first sentence of a future work comes to me. [...] When I sit in front of the empty screen, the work is basically completely formed inside of me, even though it is not at a conscious level. But somewhere beneath the threshold of consciousness, it already exists and it's only necessary to type it out. [...] The more experienced I am as a writer, the more importance I lend to the unconscious. There lies forever preserved everything I ever experienced, everything I've seen, heard, read, learned... The unconscious is like a place in which fermentation is constantly ongoing, but the turmoil reigning there is only ostensibly chaotic. At the moment when a certain critical mass is reached, from the turbulence of the unconscious a thread of a new work begins to be woven, and it is perfectly composed."[20]

Someone can be an excellent writer without ever attempting to understand what exactly is happening behind the mysterious curtain of inspiration, in the same sense that someone can be an excellent driver without ever wondering how an internal combustion engine works. If, however, a writer wishes to teach creative writing, then they must be—in the spirit of the just mentioned comparison—if not an automobile mechanic, then at least someone who has occasionally raised the hood. True, they will teach the participants in the course or program to drive a car, not to repair it, but the teacher must at least have a general idea of what is going on under the hood. If they understand the hood as a cover beneath which something mystical is going on, they will be just a guru, not a mentor.

---

[20]Ibid., pp. 87–88.

In addition to a certain understanding of the process by which an artistic work comes about, the writer who is supposed to teach creative writing at the university also needs to have an education in literature. This is required even formally: without a doctorate they cannot deliver lectures at the university. However, there is another, even more important reason. Without the appropriate education, the writer will be unable to interpret professionally for the students the many aspects of the literary work, from the linguistic and grammatical to the stylistic and narrative. The metaphor about the car's hood is again in force here, only beneath it now is not the mechanism of inspiration, but the structure of the literary work. A writer can be a good driver even though they are unable to explain that structure, but the creative writing lecturer is expected to have an automobile mechanic's training in this regard, although their task is in no way to educate new mechanics.

If one considers what is expected of an academic creative writing mentor—to be a successful writer with a high formal literary education for whom the creation of a literary work is not just a mystical secret—it is no wonder that European universities, as opposed to their American counterparts, find creative writing staff in short supply. Yet, wherever they are at work, new writers are formed, and not new creative writing experts who are not writers themselves.

1.4   My Course in the Creative Writing of Literary Prose

I began teaching the creative writing of literary prose at the Faculty of Philology, University of Belgrade, in the autumn of 2007. At the beginning the course was one year long, but by 2008 it had become a two-year course.

Formally, it was one semester long, so that students received grades four times—for Creative Writing 1, 2, 3, and 4. In order to attend one of the higher levels, it was necessary to finish all the preceding ones.

In preparing the course, I made two strategic decisions. First of all, I defined the goal of the course. It certainly was not to create writers. Not a single mentor of creative writing has ever managed to do such a thing in all the nine and a half decades of the academic history of this subject—because it is simply impossible.

What does that mean, "create a writer," anyway? When does someone who is trying to write become a writer? After their first published book? Some of my students published their first work of fiction written under my tutelage, but that still did not make them into writers. The question is whether they would continue writing at all. There are many more of them who, after their first book, gave up on writing than those who have seen their second book published. It is actually the second book of prose that is the watershed. There are many more of those who went on writing after their second published book than those who quit writing then.

In addition, there are the optimal years for the creation of prose, and I had already warned the students of that in the introductory lecture. Perhaps I exaggerated a bit when I told them that a writer does not come into existence before the age of fifty, and that they should not expect immediate success in prose writing. However, there is no doubt that a writer's maturity, that which is necessary for someone to be truly called a writer, is not attained in one's student years.

The purpose of my course in the creative writing of literary prose was to enable students to write better. By this, at the beginning I meant the improvement of their general ability to articulate their thoughts in written form.

Although I directed them toward writing stories in the very first class, we dealt very little with prose during the first semester. My initial instructions dealt with writing in general. I tutored them first in grammar, and then in how to compose, coherently, consistently and clearly, a complete text.

In an ideal world, one would expect students who choose a course in creative writing as an elective subject already to have a command of these basic skills, in the same way that, for example, students at a music academy enrolled in a course on composition would be expected to know musical notes and to have an ear. In the real world, however, students also apply for a course in creative writing who are not only alarmingly unfamiliar with the notes of prose, but are also quite lacking an ear for it. These shortcomings must at least be diluted, if not removed, before one begins to approach the composition of prose, and at least one semester is spent so doing.

Only then does it make sense to move from the terrain of general literacy to the particular terrain of prose. Three semesters later, the course was not finished by fully formed writers, but by students who were more skilful in writing at the end than they were at the beginning. Those who are especially talented and persistent—a minority by the very nature of things—will perhaps go on to write prose, inspired by the teaching and support they received from me, so that one day some of them actually become writers. The rest will certainly make some use of having learned to write better, regardless of what they end up doing. In both cases, the goal of the creative writing course will be reached.

The second strategic decision was related to the way the course was held. I had two approaches available, of which one could be called deconstructionist, and the second holistic. The first presupposes that a work of prose is a conglomerate creation that can be disassembled into its constituent parts, so that they can later be treated separately. In the framework of the second approach, the work of prose is considered to be an amalgam which is greater than the sum of its constituent parts, and therefore it is not disassembled.

The deconstructive approach is dominant in contemporary courses and programs of creative writing in the English-speaking world. It also has adherents among the teachers of creative writing in Europe. The course of the Slovene writer and professor Andrej Blatnik, for example, is based on that approach, as explained in his book *Short Story Writing: from First Draft to Publication.*

Professor Blatnik decomposes the story, which is the subject of study in his course, into as many as forty-four constituent units which are individually treated. Here are those units: of what do we speak when we speak about writing, the beginnings of writing, the short story, of what do we not speak when we speak about writing, "I would write, but I can't get started", ideas, going beyond oneself, materials, three degrees of writing, the beginning, characters, characterizations, narrator, unreliable narrator, dialogue, monologue, space, time, point of view, multiple points of view, change of view, different view, structure, plot, narration and description, blanks, compacting, style, five senses, brands, endings, title, the whole is more than the sum of its parts, attitude, influences, sharpening, common mistakes, writer's block, reader, empowering, how to get published, driving direction, who narrates, writers' groups and how to survive them.[21]

Work on most of these constituent parts is completed with exercises. Participants in Professor Blatnik's course are

---

[21] *Short Story Writing: from First Draft to Publication*, pp. 5–6.

tasked with practicing the writing of the individual parts of a story—the idea, the beginning, the plot, the characters, the point of view and narrative flow, the ending, and so on. Only after becoming skilled in the composition of those individual parts do they undertake the uniting of such acquired experience in the writing of a story as a whole.

As opposed to this, the holistic approach which I prefer does not presuppose any sort of preparatory work for the writing of a story. At the very first class I tasked my students with writing a story, convinced that they could do so even though they had had no training from me. The majority of these stories were full of beginners' shortcomings, but they were satisfactory in one essential aspect: they were indubitably a narrative text.

I am convinced that most people attain the ability to compose a narrative at a very early age, and that it is much like the learning of language. Just as language is learned without any sort of understanding about its grammatical and linguistic aspects, so the telling of stories is mastered without any sort of teaching about the complex composition of a narrative. When a little one who has recently begun to talk tells their parents about an experience, and also spices it up with an imaginary addition, the child is acting as a narrator for the first time. The parents usually make a big mistake here—they scold the child for making things up. Thus, without meaning to, they actually hinder the budding writer in the child, whose artistry is in fact founded on the ability to imagine things.

Grammatical and linguistic knowledge are not necessary even for a grownup to speak well. If they want to be more eloquent, then they should seek the help of a teacher of rhetoric, not a grammarian or a linguist. To turn once again to my comparison with the automobile, one can be a good driver all one's life and never peep under the hood. If one wants to be a better driver, then the help of a driving instructor is sought, not a mechanic. In the same way, one can be a good writer without studying literature. If one wishes to be a better writer, then help should be sought from a creative writing instructor who is also a writer, and not a literature professor who is not.[22]

Both professors of creative writing—the one using the deconstructionist approach and the one using the holistic one—teach their students to drive the prose automobile; the first foundationally practices all elements of driving a car before taking their student on their first ride, while the latter immediately takes them into traffic. The holistic teacher relies on the narrative abilities of the student—no matter how meagre they might be—attained in earliest childhood, while the deconstructionist does not have much faith in that young narrator.

My holistic approach is based on my own experience as an author. I became a writer without the preparation applied in the deconstructionist courses. I did not practice the individual elements of the whole of a prose work, nor did I compose any sort of writing outline. Instead of such an approach, which presupposes that the creation of prose is basically a rational, conscious act that is practiced and planned, all my works of prose have come from my subconscious.

Even though I have no insight into how prose comes to fruition in the subconscious, I can pick out elements of it from my own works. In them, I recognize many

---

[22]It certainly does not follow from this that knowledge of literature is wasted on a writer, although it will not help them to write better as such. (If it did, many literature teachers would be writers, and such people are rare, and actually the good ones among them are even rarer.) An automobile driver is also not harmed by knowledge of mechanics, although it does not help them to drive better. Knowledge is never harmful, even when it has no practical use.

influences that have formed me as a writer. They are primarily the traces of books I have read and the reflections of knowledge about literature that I have gathered at various times, but they are also fragments of a variety of other related experiences. All of that, together with matters that are completely new, make up the amalgam of my works of prose.

These were actually the influences that were the main stronghold in my work with students. Those influences guided me in weaving their formation as writers. I had to suppose that the things which were useful to me could be useful to them as well. And vice versa. I had to avoid those things which were of no help to me, even though they are often used in other creative writing courses.

This is primarily related to the so-called rules of writing. These are especially popular in non-academic creative writing courses in the English-speaking world. The above mentioned Gotham Writers' Workshop in New York used to have a "writers' recommendation" list of some fifteen "masters" on its website.[23] Actually, the real masters of prose are only a few there—four at the most: Edgar Allan Poe, George Orwell, Kurt Vonnegut, and Michael Moorcock, except that Poe never wrote any sort of writing rules, but they have been extracted from his works. The rest on the list are commercially successful writers of popular literature.

These "recommendations" are offered to course participants, actually, as rules that should, if they are followed, make it possible for them to write good books by themselves. Emulate the masters—that could be Gotham's

---

[23]http://www.writingclasses.com/InformationPages/index.php/PageID/269—last accessed March 19th, 2019.

slogan. If you base your works on the same rules they did, it is quite probable that you will be equally successful.

If this analogy were true, the life of a prose writer would become quite easy. That, unfortunately, is not the case. Let us consider, for example, one of the oldest collections of such recommendations in English—the "Six Rules of Great Writing" of George Orwell. This is the advice Orwell gave to inexperienced writers in 1946.

1. Never use a metaphor, simile, or other figure of speech which you are used to seeing in print.

2. Never use a long word where a short one will do.

3. If it is possible to cut a word out, always cut it out.

4. Never use the passive where you can use the active.

5. Never use a foreign phrase, a scientific word, or a jargon word if you can think of an everyday English equivalent.

6. Break any of these rules sooner than say anything outright barbarous.[24]

Orwell's advice is certainly not to be ignored. Any writer who follows it will make fewer mistakes. However, they are1j1 not enough to write a good work of prose. You can respect them completely and still have your story turn out weak. Orwell himself was aware of this. That's where the last, sixth rule came from, setting the boundaries valid for the previous five.

Sixty years before Orwell, in 1885, the idea of "rules for beginning writers" was first addressed by one of the greatest storytellers of all time, Anton Pavlovich Chekhov, with a prose text bearing precisely that title. The parody-like tone of the text and its main point embodied in

---

[24]George Orwell, "Politics and the English Language." In *Horizon*, April 1946, p. 257.

the leitmotif "Don't write!" strike at the very essence of the problem. There is no collection of rules, no matter how long, which will guarantee the creation of a good piece of literature.

The very idea of rules is contradictory to the nature of an artistic prose work. Rules are limiting by definition, and artistic creations resist such boundaries above all. Their obligatory significance is always just relative. Even when they seem to be irrefutable, it is possible to write a work of prose that will be excellent, even though it betrays them in every way. In recent times, the terminology of creative writing prefers the term "recommendations" instead of "rules," but that changes essentially nothing. "Recommendations" are just an euphemism for "rules."[25]

The inadequacy of rules, however, does not imply that prose is a field where everything is allowable. On the contrary. A work of prose is an artistic creation at the highest level of complexity where nothing is random. That complexity, however, is not mathematical in nature—in other words, reducible to an algorithm. All artistic works have basic common properties, but they cannot be expressed by rules; there is no general formula for them. This simple truth significantly complicates the job of the creative writing teacher.

I was always troubled when I tried to explain to students what comprises the specific complexity of a work of prose. Mostly I would prefer to resort to a comparison, even though I was aware of its incompleteness. I would tell them to imagine that every story is embedded in a fine net of the laws of prose. If everything is all right with the

---

[25]Emma Darwin, "Twelve Tools [not rules] of Writing," (http://emmadarwin. typepad.com/thisitchofwriting/2010/12/my-ten-tools-not-rules-of-writing. html—last accessed March 19th, 2019).

work, the netting remains whole and keeps it together. If, however, something in the work is not good, then the fine weave of the netting begins to tear and the story disintegrates.

This image inevitably confused my students at first. They could imagine the netting around the story, but not what I meant by the term "laws." First they would hope that it was a set of rules that, if they learned and obeyed them, would make it possible for them to write better. However, they would quickly become unhappy when they discovered that the "laws" are not just simple instructions.

They dictate the general properties of a work of prose. A story is a complex narrative system which is characterized by wholeness, motivational consistency, individualized characters, credibility, clarity, and compactness. At its heart is an extraordinary event worth talking about, with a suitable narrative drive. Finally, the language of the story must have a high esthetic quality.

If any of these properties are disturbed, the netting around the story fails. The central problem of the creative writing of literary prose is how to instruct writers-to-be how not to endanger the netting that holds the story together.

I could have approached this after the model of a professor of the theory of literature—to interpret generally the above-mentioned properties, hoping that the students would manage to apply that theoretical knowledge to the practice of writing. However, experience has taught me that transferring that knowledge into a work of prose is quite difficult. The libraries are full of the so-called literary works of professors that no one reads simply because they are not good. Knowledge, of course, does no harm to the writers' calling, but it is not their main stronghold.

The alternative to theoretical interpretation which I favored was explanation based on a "living text." I relied on experience here as well. Those whom I was training in writing received my mentorship best when it was based on a consideration of their own texts. I managed to explain even the most complex properties of the literary work by pointing out their mistakes in writing and suggesting ways to correct them. Knowledge received this way has the greatest practical value.

In order to provide enough material for this kind of work, students were required to write one story each month during the semester, that is, six stories during the first year of attending my course. There was also one story for their exam, making seven altogether. I required as many stories from my students during the second year as well.

In the first year, I gave the students a topic for each story. They had at least three weeks to write a story that was to be no more than five thousand characters with spaces in length. They wrote at home and sent it to me by email. When I had gathered them all in, I emailed all the stories to all the students. They would print them out and bring them to class. I too would print them out and then correct them, adding my suggestions.

During class, I read and commented on the stories. My corrections and suggestions were noted not only by the author of the given work, but also by the other students. In creative writing, one learns mostly from one's own experience, but also from the experiences of others. As opposed to the large majority of creative writing courses, no discussion was held on the stories read in mine. When this bothered a certain student one time, I joked about it, telling her that it was so because my classes are ruled by enlightened absolutism—and I am the enlightened absolutist.

The real reason no discussion was held was because it wouldn't be purposeful. Students are generally not familiar enough with literature to offer meritorious value judgments, so a discussion about the stories would quickly turn into an exchange of personal impressions, which is certainly not wanted in creative writing. I was obliged to protect young writers who, by the very nature of things, are rather sensitive to what is said about their work. I myself had to be quite careful when I was forced to make comments—they had to be composed so as to give the students no reason at all to be offended. It would be difficult, however, for their peers, even with the best intentions, to be delicate enough in this sense.

Of course, this certainly does not mean that, in spite of the enlightened absolutism, there was no democracy or free thinking in my classes. So, if someone not in the know were to have stopped by at the door of the classroom where my creative writing class was in progress, they would have been confused. They might have thought, from the laughter that often broke out, that a merry band was being entertained inside.

I stimulated an atmosphere of laughter and brightness firstly because writing and the things related to it should be joyful, and certainly not depressing and tortuous. In addition, laughter is the best defense against over-sensitivity. If I could help a student laugh or at least smile at a clumsy turn of phrase or mistake, they surely would not feel offended. Ultimately, laughter was, in general, a guarantee that I had explained something well. This is an old pedagogical trick: teaching through entertainment. Whenever I managed to make students laugh with some sort of funny example or anecdote (and I tried to make them as plentiful as possible) I was certain that most of them understood the essence of what I was trying to interpret for them.

Along with the topic I assigned them, I always read them one of my stories as well. (With the more complex topics in the second semester, I often read two or even three stories of mine.) The story was meant to give them a model that they could hold on to as much as they liked. They could write a variation on my story or wander from it completely under the same topic. I read my own stories, also, because that seemed fair on my part. Along with being a professor, I am also a writer, and it would not be fair for me to expect my students to do something I myself haven't attempted. For the same reason, I didn't use the stories of other writers as models.

Here are the six topics I assigned in the first year of my creative writing course: a conversation between the writer and the devil, a pastiche of Sherlock Holmes, an eccentric collector, estranged memory, non-linear narrative geometry, and the fantastic library. (The students would choose one of these themes to do again in their seventh and final exam story.) I would illustrate these themes with my own stories: "The Telephone," "Sherlock Holmes' Last Case: The Letter," "Fingernails," "Lost Illusions," "The First Loop," and "Home Library." The themes were chosen so as to refer to those elements of prose writing which the students needed to address first. Each of the themes has special challenges, and the three introductory ones have mitigating circumstances.

In the conversation between the writer and the devil, as it is presented in my story, the mitigation is the fact that there are only two characters, who do not have to be visually presented. Namely, the devil does not appear on the scene, and the writer is the narrator, which frees him of the obligation to describe himself. The ambient is also simple: an ordinary study. There are three challenges within the first theme: skillfully to hold a dialog whose central points are some of the essential ambiguities of literary creation, to introduce convincingly a supernatural protagonist, and to individualize the characters through speech alone.

The overall mitigation in the writing of a pastiche are the givens: the protagonists (in the case of Sherlock Holmes, there are Doyle's famous detective, his sidekick Doctor Watson, and the housekeeper Mrs. Hudson), and the setting (London at the end of the nineteenth century). It is also a convenience that I do not expect the students to write a complete story, but only the first chapter of an imaginary greater whole (what I read to them as a model is also the first chapter of a greater whole, not imaginary but already written),[26] so that they have quite a lot of freedom in creating the plot, since they do not have to resolve it in the end. The main challenge lies in dealing with at least three characters—and even more if possible—who are simultaneously on the prose stage and none of whom should be just a stand-in.

In the eccentric collector there is only one character, the creation of whom is, however, quite demanding. The students really have to exert themselves to conjure up and present an oddball preoccupied with collecting something extremely bizarre. (In my story, this is his own fingernails.) This is an excellent exercise in building a markedly individualized character. The eccentricity of the collector has a high literary value. It is not just an ordinary oddity but a complex, although benign psychological disturbance which, along with the other elements, offers the writer an opportunity for subtle comic characterization.

Estranged memory is a conceptual problem for the students. A memory which is no longer profoundly personal, for example, becomes merchandise which can be

---

[26]"Sherlock Holmes' Last Case: The Letter" is the first chapter of a lengthy pastiche of Sherlock Holmes from my novel *The Fourth Circle*.

traded (as in my story), presupposing a public approach to an otherwise inaccessible intimacy. This opens up the possibility for an essentially new class of plots. Estranged memory is an excellent training ground for exercising inventiveness in prose.

The theme I call "non-linear narrative geometry" is the most complex challenge with which I confronted the students. They were required to create a seemingly perfectly realistic prose world which, however, contains a paradoxical feature, like those which appear in the drawings of Maurits Cornelis Escher. Their model for this was the first part of four from my novel *Escher's Loops*, where a series of episodes forms an apparently impossible circular narrative, which still does not make the invented reality any less convincing. In order to achieve this, an above average imagination in prose is necessary.

Finally, the fantastic library is a theme of the highest order in prose because it appears in some of the most remarkable works of world literature. I gave it as the sixth and last, so that students would have a chance, in writing it, to use everything they had already learned in my course. After listening to my story in class, I recommended that they also read others from my suite *The Library*, and certainly a few of those from other authors, above all Borges' "The Library of Babel." In the story of the fantastic library, the students were supposed to show that they had mastered the basic craftsmanship of prose writing, thus demostrating their originality for the first time, and proving they were ready for the second year of the creative writing course.

The roughly two hundred stories that I considered, corrected and commented upon with the students during the first year of the creative writing course, were a sufficiently broad training ground for exercising those qualities I indicated as the main properties of a work of prose: wholeness,

motivational consistency, individualized characters, credibility, clarity, compactness, narrative drive, and highly
esthetic language.

After the first two semesters, my students were in no
way fully-fledged writers, but most of them where capable
of writing a story mature enough for publication, which is
perhaps the best measure of the success of a creative writing course. This was practically confirmed in the spring
of 2012 when, in order to refresh the course, I decided to
change the sixth topic. Instead of the story about the fantastic library, I tasked the students with writing an erotic
story.

I warned them that I had given them an enormous
challenge in so doing: this is one of the most difficult
themes in prose. It turned out, however, that they were
ready for it. As many as twenty-five of the thirty-two students wrote a surprisingly good story. Some insignificant
polishing was necessary—but in no way could one con-
clude that the stories came from the pens of authors who
had been complete beginners only half a year earlier. These
twenty-five stories entered the contents of the anthology
Eros at the Faculty of Philology, which made a most appropriate culmination to the first year of my course.[27]

The second year of the course could be taken by students who had obtained the highest grades (nines and
tens) in the first year. This selection was justified, since
I raised the prose c   rossbar rather above the level of
the short story. It was necessary to write a mosaic novel—a
collection of seven stories, with an unlimited length, each
of them apparently being stand-alone, with the final story
gathering them all into a whole greater than the sum of

---

[27] *Eros na filološkom [Eros at the Faculty of Philology]*, Zavod za udžbenike,
Beograd, 2012.

its constituent parts. The mosaic novel, of course, does not necessarily have seven parts. I chose this number in the second year so that I could maintain the tempo of one story per month, along with the combinatory story as the final exam.

As a model for the mosaic novel, there were ten of my works of this type available to my students: *Time Gifts, Impossible Encounters, Seven Touches of Music, The Library, Steps through the Mist, Twelve Collections, Four Stories till the End, The Bridge, Miss Tamara the Reader,* and *Amarcord.* The number of connected stories in these works is in a range of three to twelve. At the end of the first year, I gave a set of these books to each of my students who intended to continue my course so that they could read them over the summer vacation and thus prepare for the second year.

The mosaic novel is a suitable form for the second half of a creative writing course. This is a novel-like structure, but seemingly a bit less tight-knit than a novel which is a monolithic whole. The students had the impression that they were doing the same tasks as in the first year, but I was there to warn them constantly to keep track of the many aspects which previously, in the writing of unrelated stories, they did not have to take into account. The most important of them was that every stroke of the prose paintbrush had to be measured from two aspects— the aspect of the given story and that of the whole of the mosaic novel.

The main job at the beginning of the third semester was to establish the framework for the whole, to get as complete as possible an idea about the general outline of the work. This significantly eased the writing of individual stories because it made possible the above-mentioned sizing up from two aspects. Actually, in creating the framework of the whole I was perhaps able to contribute most as a mentor. My voluminous experience in working on mosaic novels helped me to pick out those of highest potential in the vague ideas of the whole which the students had at the beginning.

Also in the second year, I reminded my students frequently of the main properties of a work of prose. I wanted to build up a kind of conditional reflex in them which would drive them to be extremely careful about those properties once they became independent. In addition, the longer form gave me the opportunity to teach them some of the properties of the prose text which were not elaborated upon in the first year because they do not often appear in short stories. These are, for example, episodes, digressions, leitmotifs, rhythms, cadences... Here as well there were no shortcuts. There are no simple rules that this set of properties can be reduced to, but, as with the primary ones, the students needed to be instructed using the "living text."

My course in the writing of literary prose did not end in the mere assigning of grades. Grading itself was, for me, always secondary. As I said, I did not fail students, even in those rare cases when they deserved it. And they deserved it not because they were not talented at writing prose—I would never punish someone for that—but because of their lack of motivation to learn anything from me, though I did my best to inspire them.

My grades were not important because they did not make anyone into a writer. The highest grade from me meant, in fact, that I had spotted certain qualities that indicated the literary potential of a student: talent, readiness to learn, persistence, being well-read... The highest grade, however, was no sort of guarantee that this potential would be further developed. A writer comes into being only with a published work. And, as mentioned before, not just the first one, but the second...

Yet, the first one is also important. Without it, there is no second, no graduation. And the publishing situation has never been favorable for writers-to-be. Not a single commercial publisher is bursting with enthusiasm to publish the work of an anonymous author, especially not a local writer. I could hardly be blamed if I just shrugged my shoulders at those conditions. No one could expect me to improve them.

Still, if I had remained indifferent and passive, the objections would arrive from a place I couldn't possibly ignore—from my own conscience. It would seem to me that I had turned my back on my students at the critical moment. I had brought them to the last step in the long and in no way easy procedure of creating a work of prose, and once they had written it, I just let them find their own way in the market horror of the book industry. I had to do something about that.

A solution to the problem appeared in the offer of one of the few remaining non-commercial publishers in Serbia. Belgrade's Institute for Textbooks agreed in 2010 to accept my proposal to start up a series called "Young Voices," where the works of my students could appear. This was wonderful both for my students and for my course which, in spite all my efforts to make it as good as possible, would remain incomplete without this final touch—without the opportunity for the fruits of creative writing to see the light of day. Indeed, is there a better way to establish the value of a creative writing course than to read the books that were created by it?

In the "Young Voices" series, only four books appeared. Even though there were at least two highest grades at the end of the course every year, they did not mean that the work which earned them deserved to be published. For that even more was necessary—the highest grade plus one, as I usually told my students. The highest grade is given by a professor who has the right to be benevolent and ignore some of the imperfections of a mosaic novel. A high grade plus one is given by an editor who must be guided by only one factor. Five years after a book comes out, the author, who has in the meantime become well-known, mustn't have a reason to reproach their professor for having recommended their weakest work for publication…

I was not the only one who gave grades in the creative writing course. At the end of the second semester my students also offered their grades. They evaluated my overall work on the usual scale from 5 to 10. They could also grade me descriptively.

One of those descriptive grades is especially dear to me.

"Dear Professor, at the beginning of your course I felt like an unshaped clay writer. Now I have a shape. Thank you so much."

The students had the privilege of not signing their grades, their evaluations. They gave them sheltered by the comfort of anonymity, which is only right. Because of that, I will never know to whom I owe the title of this book.

Translated from the Serbian by Randall Major.

2

Annotations 1

The Clay Writer: Shaping in Creative Writing was originally published as *Pisac od gline: Oblikovati u kreativnom pisanju* in 2013 by The Faculty of Philology, University of Belgrade. It was at that time only the second book ever written by a Serbian academic about creative writing. This subject was introduced in one of the Serbian universities in 2004.

The original edition of *The Clay Writer* is somewhat longer than the English language Springer edition you are currently reading. The first part of the book in Serbian contains a broad overview entitled "A Brief History of Creative Writing". It was omitted from this volume because it refers mostly to the academic history of creative writing in the USA, about which there are extensive primary sources written by American scholars. Although my text could certainly be informative and interesting for readers as a reliable recapitulation, it is inevitably somewhat less original than the rest of the first part of my book.

© Springer Nature Switzerland AG 2019
Z. Živković, *The Clay Writer*,
https://doi.org/10.1007/978-3-030-19753-7_2

The second part of the Serbian edition of *The Clay Writer* is in fact an appendix to the main body of the book. Its principal ingredients are my own pieces of fiction, but there are also a few other items related to creative writing that I found relevant and useful or particularly amusing. Examples of the latter are two excellent humoresques: "Rules for Aspiring Writers" by Anton Pavlovich Chekhov and "When I started to write…" by Jaroslav Hašek.

Although I would love to see both of them included in this volume, they were omitted because it seemed appropriate to stick to the form applied in my first Springer book, *First Contact and Time Travel: Selected Essays and Short Stories* (2018). The second, "fiction" part of the book should contain only my own stories. Fortunately, Chekhov's and Hašek's humoresques are easily available elsewhere and I do recommend them wholeheartedly to your attention.

The same principle required that a piece of mine was also excluded from the second part of the Springer edition of *The Clay Writer*. Not being fictional, my brief, confessional essay "How I Write" would be a foreign body among my stories. I remain hopeful, however, that this is not my last Springer book and that in some future volume an appropriate place might be found for what is probably my most introspective text so far…

ZORAN ŽIVKOVIĆ

PISAC od GLINE

OBLIKOVATI U KREATIVNOM PISANJU

Zoran Živković

PISAC od GLINE

Part II
Fiction

3

The Telephone

When the telephone rang I shot up in my chair.

In the still of the night this sudden sound seemed almost like a clap of thunder. Roused out of my reveries, in my initial confusion I could only stare in disbelief at the telephone on my desk, as though seeing it for the first time. The second ring made me snap out of this suspended animation. As I quickly reached for the receiver, almost in fear, I glanced at the lower right hand corner of the monitor in front of me, where four numbers showed the time. That was the only writing on the empty white screen. It was 47 min after midnight.

I had no idea who could be calling so late. Certainly not an acquaintance, because everyone knows I work at night and no one would want to disturb me. Unless, of course, something had happened that couldn't wait until morning, in which case it surely would not be something nice. Nonetheless, I hoped it wasn't some kind of trouble. Someone had probably dialed the wrong number. That happened every once in a while, although never before at

© Springer Nature Switzerland AG 2019
Z. Živković, *The Clay Writer*,
https://doi.org/10.1007/978-3-030-19753-7_3

this late hour. Who in the world would think of making a call after midnight? And then pay no attention to the number they'd dialed? People can be so inconsiderate.

I put the receiver to my ear and said sharply, "Hello!"

"Good evening!" said someone at the other end of the line. I'd been certain it would be a young person, most likely under the influence of a substance that had put them in a very happy mood. Instead I heard the deep, serious voice of a middle-aged man, so my hackles came down a little. I'd been ready to deliver a tirade on bad manners to the unknown young caller, but now I just replied, "Good evening," although still in a surly tone.

"This is the Devil," said the man evenly, just like one of my friends saying who was calling.

I sat there speechless for several moments and then hung up the phone. I was ready to understand that someone had called the wrong number in the middle of the night, but to call me intentionally just to play a joke, and an adult to boot! What had the world come to?

The moment I put the receiver down the phone rang again. This time I didn't wait for the idle prankster to say anything, but was quite blunt.

"If you don't stop disturbing me this instant I'll call the phone company and have them put a trace on you. Then you'll have to pay a hefty fine for what you're doing and you might even end up in jail. Aren't you ashamed of such behavior at your age?"

"How can you put a trace on the Devil? If you call the phone company they'll say you didn't have any calls. That would put you in a really tight spot. What could you say to explain the fact that you reported annoying calls that never happened?"

The stranger clearly did not intend to give up. Fine, I had a remedy for that. I slammed down the receiver, which was unnecessary since it couldn't be heard at the other end of the line, but it let me vent my feelings a bit. Then I felt for the button on the back of the phone that turned off the sound and pushed it. There! How convenient. If only it were possible to remove other problems by simply pushing a button. Now how would he be able to continue his nasty game?

I saw soon enough. Or rather heard. The telephone rang again.

At first I thought I hadn't pushed the right button. There are several of them and I don't use them very often, so I might have made a mistake. Letting the phone ring, I picked it up, turned it around, checked which of the buttons turned off the sound and pushed hard, which was also uncalled for since it reacts to the slightest touch. Nothing happened. The sound continued to echo sharply at regular intervals. I pushed the button again quickly another four or five times, with no result. The only possibility I could think of was that the button was broken. What else? I stared at the phone briefly, not knowing what to do. Every new wave of relentless ringing irritated me more and more. I had to do something as soon as possible. So I did the simplest, although not the wisest, thing. I lifted the receiver again, knowing that I was playing into the hands of a crank. Never strike up a conversation with a psychopath because it will lead to no good.

"Listen, you…" I started, but the deep voice interrupted me.

"Did you really expect to turn off the Devil with a button?"

When I slammed down the receiver again, I was spurred not only by the same irritation as the first time but also by the icy fingers of fear that suddenly grabbed my chest. I tried to convince myself that it had been easy for him to guess what I'd done because anyone in my place would have tried that first, but this explanation did not seem quite convincing. Feeling a shudder slide down my spine, I promptly got up from my desk, went around it, bent down and with a deep sigh pulled the telephone cord out of the wall socket.

The relief was short-lived. As I was returning to my chair, the telephone rang again. I stopped dead in my tracks, turned around and fixed my eyes on the disconnected cord. I then spent several moments with my eyes riveted to the telephone as it did something it certainly should not be doing. I might have stood there even longer without moving but the ringing seemed to be getting louder each time. Before long the apartments around me would hear it and the last thing I needed was for noise from my study to wake up the neighbors. I had no choice.

I picked up the receiver slowly, waited a bit and then said softly, "Hello?"

"Have you finally come to your senses?" said the same voice reprovingly. "It's simply unbelievable how long it takes people to accept something as innocuous as a telephone call from the Devil. Just imagine what would happen if the Devil himself turned up on your doorstep. Indeed, to be fair, you were quite quick about it, but sometimes it drags on and on. And is unpleasant. Some behave quite imprudently. In their stubborn refusal to confront reality, they sometimes even throw the telephone out the window on the top floor of a building. And then the Devil is to blame when the phone, broken to smithereens, keeps ringing so loudly that it causes panic throughout the neighborhood. But there is no other way. Some people can't be treated with kid gloves."

There was a short lull before I spoke again. My voice was still disconsolate.

"What do you want from me?"

"From you? Nothing."

I hesitated once again.

"Then why did you call me?"

"I was only returning your call."

"My call?" I repeated, flabbergasted, collapsing back in the chair.

"Yes, yours. Didn't you think just a moment ago that you would willingly make a pact with the Devil, anything just so you didn't have to look at the empty screen in front of you? To get some inspiration?"

I swallowed the lump in my throat. I thought of asking him how he knew what had been on my mind, then realized the question was out of place. He probably wouldn't have answered me anyway.

Instead I said, "But that was just figurative…metaphorical. I didn't mean it literally."

"Is that so? It didn't look that way to me. Does that mean you don't need my services?"

I had to say right away that I didn't. Even though my heart was pounding wildly and my ears were ringing, I still had enough of my wits about me to reason properly. You should never find yourself in cahoots with the Devil.

When I took my time answering and then said, "I do, but their price—?" it seemed to be coming out of someone else's mouth.

"Everything has its price."

"My soul?" I asked almost in a whisper.

"What hogwash. Who needs a writer's soul? And a failed one to boot."

Although this should have been a relief, it felt like a pin had suddenly been jabbed in my backside.

"Well then, what?" I replied somewhat more forcefully. My wounded pride brought back a bit of self-confidence.

"I'll take great pleasure in your torments."

"What torments?" My voice softened again.

"Mental, of course. What else? You will agonize."

"Oh, that's it." I didn't say anything for a moment, then added reluctantly, "What will I agonize over?"

"What you will be denied."

"What will I be denied?"

"Success during your lifetime or a place in literary history. The choice is up to you."

"I can choose between those two things?"

"Yes. Take your pick. If you want to be considered a great writer in the history of literature, that will be possible, but only posthumously. You will be neglected and opposed during your lifetime. Almost no one will read you. This will make you first wrathful and frustrated, convinced that a great injustice is being done to you. Then you'll start to doubt yourself, you'll slowly lose the desire to write, you'll sink deeper and deeper into despair, and in the end you might even take your own life. Actually, I hope you do. Such an outcome is the best compensation for my services."

"Why would I take my own life when I know that after my death I'll be recognized as a great writer?"

"Are you sure you would find that enough solace? In any case, what kind of guarantee would you have?"

"Our pact, of course. Your word." My voice trembled slightly.

"Many would roar with laughter if they heard that you trusted the Devil's word. Mind you, I always abide by the pacts I make."

"All right, and the other possibility?"

"You'll be very popular. You will be highly read and thereby famous. Probably rich too. Deluded by success, you won't take much notice of the fact that experts refuse to see any kind of literary value in your books. At least not in the beginning. As the years pass, however, this lack of recognition will get harder and harder to bear. The certainty that you will be quickly forgotten as a writer will force you to feel disillusioned, ineffectual, a failure. That will probably not be enough for you to commit suicide—quite a shame, of course—but the suffering will be long lasting."

I didn't know what to reply. We sank into a tense silence.

"That's not much of a choice," I said at last.

"Perhaps, but you shouldn't complain. You at least are able to choose. There are so many writers who are never given the chance to make any kind of choice, even though they call upon me, just like you. Some on a daily basis and some even several times a day. But you can't please everyone, that's clear. Where would that lead us? They are left without success during their lifetime and without a place in literary history."

Something suddenly crossed my mind. "But some writers are successful during their lifetime and achieve a distinguished place in the history of literature. What about them? I mean, what kind of choice did you offer them?"

"None. They simply didn't need my help, so they didn't call upon me. Someone else was their benefactor, unfortunately."

The telephone line went silent once more.

I was the first to break it again. "Do I have to tell you my choice right away?"

"No. You don't have to say a thing about it. I'll have no trouble establishing what you've decided as soon as you start to write. Everything will be crystal clear."

I sighed. "But that's just the problem. How can I start to write when nothing comes? Would we even be having this conversation if that weren't true?"

"Well, we can solve that problem at least. Write a story about our conversation."

"About our conversation?" I repeated, bewildered. "But I don't write horror stories."

"Is this a horror story?" The tone of his voice seemed tinged with insult and anger.

"No, of course not," I said, hastening to repair the damage. "But you know, the Devil appears…"

"It doesn't have to be literal. Make it figurative, metaphorical."

"It would still be fantasy."

"Do you have something against fantasy?" That same tone of voice.

"No, not at all. I've just never tried it. But, why not? I might give it a crack…"

"There, you see. I suggest that you get right down to work while your impressions are still fresh."

"Of course." I paused. "I suppose I ought to thank you…"

"Don't thank me. Right now this seems like a great service, but in the end you'll curse me for it. And don't call me anymore. It would come to nothing. I only appear once."

"I understand," I replied. "Then, God speed."

I bit my tongue, but it was too late. Before the connection broke, a sound reached my ear resembling a growl, but somehow huskier, more ominous. I hurriedly hung up the phone.

My compulsion for tidiness urged me to put the telephone cord back in the socket where it belonged, but I didn't. It could stay there disconnected, despite the fact that there would be no more unexpected night calls. Even so, when I typed the first sentence of 'The Telephone' at the top of the empty screen—*When the telephone rang I shot up in my chair*—I could have sworn that my ears filled with a sharp, piercing sound.

Translated from the Serbian by Alice Copple Tošić.

4

Sherlock Holmes' Last Case: The Letter

"What do you think of this, Watson?"

Holmes extended to me an opened envelope. It departed from the standards of the Royal Mail: elongated and bluish, it had a rectangular, not triangular, flap on its reverse side. There was no stamp or any trace of a postmark. On the front were inscribed Holmes's name and address, in neat, gently slanting handwriting with something of a tendency to ornamentation. The sender had made no effort to leave any trace of his own identity.

Not wishing to disappoint my friend, who in circumstances like this always goodheartedly expects that I will be nearly, if not quite, as astute as he is, I held the envelope to my nose. Doing just this, he had many times gleaned precious information. I was aware of a slight, bitter smell but could not place it, though for some reason I thought of the shock to which the sense of smell is exposed upon entering a shop selling Indian spices.

Holmes looked unblinkingly at me, with that penetrating stare of his, a stare that filled even the most confident

© Springer Nature Switzerland AG 2019
Z. Živković, *The Clay Writer*,
https://doi.org/10.1007/978-3-030-19753-7_4

criminals with unease and caused the ladies to squirm uncomfortably; but he remained silent, though I noticed a slight curling of the fine lines at the corners of his mouth, which I knew indicated a barely controlled impatience.

"How did this arrive?" I asked him, taking the letter out of the envelope. It was of the same bluish tint, on stiff paper, folded in three. I did not unfold it at once.

"Somebody pushed it under the front door. Between four o'clock, when I returned from my walk, and a quarter-past six, when Mrs. Simpson went off to do the evening shopping. She did not bring it to me immediately, but only after she had returned and served my meal. She said she thought it could not be of great consequence, since it had been delivered in this manner; in truth, it was too much of an effort for her to climb the stairs to the drawing room a second time, though she would never admit it. I myself tend to breathe a little harder after those nineteen steps, especially when I take them at a run, while she is sixty-seven and arthritic, but that is unimportant. Come, open the letter."

He was right about the staircase. I could still feel my heart beating faster from the climb, as well as from my brisk walk from home. It seemed that I was not exactly young myself, but the communication from Holmes had been categorical. "Come at once! Very urgent!" Hurrying here, even running part of the way, I imagined a multitude of troubles that might have befallen him. Thank God, all it was was an unusual letter. I was careful not to say this aloud, though; it obviously had special importance for Holmes. Why else would he have called me with such urgency?

When I unfolded the stiff paper, a surprise awaited me: only a large circle was drawn on it. Nothing else was there—no text, no signature, no initials, nor, indeed, any sign at all. My first thought on perceiving the precision of the circle was that it must have been made with a pair of compasses, but when I looked more closely at the place where the center should have been, I could not see the little hole, which would inevitably have been made by the sharp point. Evidently, the drawing had been made with the assistance of some round object, probably some kitchen vessel; a largish cup, perhaps, or a saucer.

"A circle," said I rather feebly, nothing more intelligent crossing my mind.

"Excellent, my dear Watson! A circle!" replied Holmes. His voice bore no hint of ridicule, though my perspicacity had warranted it. He spoke the words as if I really had reached a brilliant conclusion.

"Someone has decided to play a prank on us, no doubt," I continued. "However, even from a prankster one would have expected something more clever than an ordinary circle."

Holmes's reaction was so strong and violent that I almost flinched back.

"Nonsense!" he exclaimed. "Balderdash! A circle is anything but ordinary! The only perfect… complete… like… like…"

Holmes was not rarely given to rages like this, but I do not remember when last I saw him speechless. What looked to me like someone's stupid joke, to him seemed, for some reason, altogether more serious. I knew from experience that at such times he should not be contradicted. Indeed, when he spoke again his voice was perfectly calm, with the usual ironic undertone that had the effect of constantly making his companion re-examine the reasonableness of what was being said.

"All right, let's leave the circle aside for the time being," said he. "We will return to it later. Observe the letter carefully and tell me what else you see."

I brought the letter and the envelope closer to my eyes and looked attentively. After a few long moments of examination, I humbly admitted, "I fail to notice anything further... The format is unusual, though. I have never seen anything like it, but from that I can deduce nothing."

"Indeed," replied Holmes. "Unusual it is, at least here in England. On the continent you will come across it more often. What does the paper tell you?"

I felt it again, more carefully. Now I gained the impression that it possessed, apart from stiffness, the quality of antiquity, a patina. For a moment it seemed to me that I held something very old, a parchment perhaps, between my fingers, though my eyes were telling me that it was a newly made sheet of paper.

"I don't know," I said finally. "It gives the impression of being somehow... foreign. Most probably it also originates from the Continent."

"Italy," responded Holmes succinctly, as if uttering the most banal of statements. He gave me no opportunity to ask him whence he obtained that knowledge, nor was any needed, as the look of puzzlement was quite clear on my face. He approached me, wordlessly took the letter from my hand, and raised it to the lamp that hung above a carved wood chest of drawers in the corner. "Look carefully," he said briefly.

The glow of the lamp flame shone through the unfolded paper. I moved two steps closer, the better to study it, so that now the flame seemed to be in the center of the circle painted on the paper, and I noticed that which Holmes wanted me to see. Brought to life by the light shining from the obverse side of the page, a large letter "M" in a rich calligraphic form appeared in the middle, but it was pale as a wraith, seen only in silhouette. When I moved a little to one side, the reflection of the flame slid towards the edge of the paper and the character disappeared.

"How…?" I asked distractedly.

"A watermark," replied Holmes, again in a disaffected tone. Then his voice regained its enthusiasm, and he started to explain. "The invisible trademark of unique craftsmanship. Only one man in the whole world produces such paper, my dear Watson, the maestro Umberto Murratori of Bologna. 'Cartefficio Murratori,' a branch of an old family of printers and publishers. The clientele for his paper is extremely select: important state offices, the Vatican, and also certain semipublic or secret societies, the Masons, for instance."

"What is so special about it? It does not seem extraordinary, except that it is rather stiff…"

"Appearances can be deceptive, Watson. Try burning it."

"What?"

Since I naturally did not try to do as he proposed, he shrugged and without hesitation put one end of the letter to the top of the gas light. Had it been ordinary paper, it would have begun to smoke and then to burn. The corner that Holmes held in his hand only curled a little; there was no sign of burning.

"You see, then, why Murratori's product is in such demand. The writing on it cannot easily be destroyed. Oh, this paper can burn too, of course, but for that to happen, a temperature far in excess of 451 °F is required. Similarly, it cannot be harmed by water—only by certain very strong acids."

"I see," said I, taking the letter again from Holmes. I touched the corner that had been exposed to the heat of the gas lamp and then jerked my hand quickly away. It was very hot. "But, indubitably, it can be destroyed by mechanical means." I added.

"Indubitably," repeated Holmes. "But it would take a very sharp knife, almost a surgeon's scalpel."

For a moment I was almost tempted to put this claim to the test by trying to tear the letter in half. I refrained, however, from such an act, partly out of respect for the mysterious document that was apparently so precious to Holmes and partly because of earlier, unpleasant experiences related to my disputing some of his other apparently absurd claims.

"This upper-class clientele, then, purchases durability from Murratori," I said. "What is written on this paper can do battle with time itself."

"Exactly so," replied Holmes. "Also, the price narrows the circle of possible buyers drastically. For the manufacture of a single sheet of this paper, several months of hard work are necessary. It is, in fact, a precious substance, more valuable even than gold to some people. No one except the master Murratori himself knows all the ingredients that go into this paper, and there are rumors that he obtains his raw materials from the Far East. They say that the secret of making this paper was brought to one of his ancestors by Marco Polo himself, from his first exploration of China, though I am of the opinion that this is an exaggeration."

"If this is all true, Holmes, then something really puzzles me. Who would be so foolish as to squander such a treasure for the dispatching of… er… trivial messages?"

For a moment it seemed to me that Holmes would again erupt in anger, and I was already beginning to bite my tongue because of my clumsily formulated thought, but his knitted eyebrows quickly relaxed again, and on his lips flickered the usual smile of superior knowledge.

"The logic of the entire affair eludes you, Watson. It is precisely the fact that the communication is written on Murratori's paper that eliminates any possibility of it being a foolish prank. No one, we can be certain, would be prepared to squander such a precious item on mere childishness. Hence we are to take this message quite seriously. The means by which it was delivered exacts that from us."

"But one would not expect that any important and, moreover, mysterious message should go unsigned. A gentleman should on no account allow himself to have a hand in any doings with anonymous letters, no matter how important they may seem to him."

Holmes eyed me suspiciously. I do not know what he thought of my sudden moralizing, but judging by the grimace that fleetingly crossed his face, the two of us hardly shared the same view of gentlemanly virtues at that moment. In any case, he found an elegant and unexpected escape from the trap that I had set for him.

"Who says the letter is unsigned?"

"What? But except for the circle, there is no other…" I exclaimed, quite at a loss.

"For Heaven's sake, Watson, isn't the signature staring you right in the face?" He feigned amazement, although he was, in fact, secretly jubilant over my confusion. Once more he took the letter from my hands, lifted it to the light, and tapped with the knuckle of his long, bony forefinger on the large letter "M" when it became visible again.

"You are not saying," said I, quite discomposed, "that Signore Murratori himself sent us this message?"

Now it was his turn to be surprised. "How did that thought cross your mind?"

"Well, it is his initial, is it not? 'M' for Murratori. The trademark, you yourself said so."

"No, no," replied Holmes, dismissing it with a wave of his hand. "You fail to comprehend. The existence of the watermark is the trademark. The letter itself is the initial of the sender."

"So, who then? Surely you do not mean the…?"

Holmes triumphantly nodded his head, without waiting for me to finish my thought. In his eyes there was now that familiar gleam that accompanies the moments when great mysteries are unraveled.

"Masons? The Freemasons, I mean?" said I, finally completing my sentence.

Lightning-fast, he turned on his heel, so that his back was to me. The sound that he made reminded me more than anything of a snarl, so that I instinctively retreated a step. Obviously I had not guessed the signatory of the letter.

He remained thus turned for a few moments more and then directed himself again at me. The previous gleam in his eyes had clouded over with the very essence of rage.

"Freemasons! That superior bunch of do-nothings and lazy-bones! Useless intriguers, utterly undeserving of…"

He bit his thin lower lip, as he always did when trying to control his wrath. When he continued, his voice was lower, though it still shook with rage.

"Please, Watson, in the name of friendship, do not ever again mention that… that breed…"

"But didn't you yourself say that they were Murratori's customers?" I said, in an attempt to justify myself.

"Watson—please!" His voice went up an octave.

"Very well, very well," I countered. "Who, then, is hiding behind that mysterious 'M'?"

Before answering he paused, sighing two or three times, obviously trying to compose himself, but also for effect. Holmes was, in fact, an unfulfilled actor.

"My evil fate," he spoke at last, in a voice so hushed that I barely registered it. "My curse. Moriarty…"

Translated from the Serbian by Mary Popović.

5

Fingernails

Mr. Prohaska collected his fingernail clippings. He'd been doing it since the age of eight, when he cut them by himself for the first time. He was so proud of the fact that he'd managed to cut them without his mother's help and without doing himself any harm that he decided to save the ten little sickles as proof of this feat. He'd had to do it in secrecy because his mother certainly wouldn't have let him keep them. He put them in a little plastic bag and stuck a label on it with the date. Letters were still giving him trouble, but at that early age he was already skilled with numbers. He then put the bag in a hidden place.

Approximately two weeks later, when the time came to cut his nails again, he hesitated but a moment before putting the new little sickles in a bag with the date on it. There was no long-term decision behind this; that would only be formed later. He simply felt it was a shame to throw the nails away. It suddenly seemed that doing so would be throwing away part of his body. True, he was no longer physically connected to the nails, but this did

© Springer Nature Switzerland AG 2019
Z. Živković, *The Clay Writer*,
https://doi.org/10.1007/978-3-030-19753-7_5

nothing to lessen his attachment to them. They might have separated from him, but he could still keep them close by. Sadness filled him at the thought of the many nails his mother had cut off before he turned eight and which were now lost forever.

He continued to collect his nails in an orderly fashion, but the passage of time brought the problem of where to put the little bags. Every year there were twenty-five to thirty more of them. The shoebox where he kept them was not easy to hide; his mother almost found it two or three times. He felt no relief until his early twenties, when he left his parents' home. His fingernail collection at that time contained more than four hundred little bags that filled all of three shoeboxes. That's when he was finally able to put it in order and go through it without the constant fear of being caught doing something unseemly, although he wasn't the slightest bit ashamed of his secret.

He did feel ashamed, however, of keeping something he cared about so much in such an unsuitable place as a shoebox. It seemed like sacrilege to him; he had to find a more dignified repository for his unique collection. Although he still wasn't earning very much money, he nonetheless managed to set aside enough to order five hundred specially fitted cigarette cases. Had he been richer, they certainly would have been made of solid silver, but under the circumstances he had to be satisfied with silver plating. Every cigarette case had a date engraved on the lid and the inside was lined in purple plush with two curved rows, each containing five sickle-shaped indentations.

It took several months to transfer the nails from the little bags to the cigarette cases. It was a tedious and exacting job. He did it with great patience, meticulously, consumed by the constant fear of getting it wrong. It was extremely difficult to ascertain the finger from which each nail had been cut. He finally got the hang of it and then all he needed was a quick touch to place a given sickle accurately in the proper indentation. He proudly considered himself a genuine expert in this type of identification.

The collection was finally lodged in a suitable repository, but one day as he gazed at it with pride an uneasy thought spoiled his pleasure. What if a burglar broke into his apartment? He would certainly head straight for the cigarette cases, particularly since there was nothing else of any value. Perhaps, in his haste, he wouldn't even check what was inside them. Later he would certainly throw away the nails because for him they had no value. This possibility horrified Mr. Prohaska; he had to prevent it at any cost. He rushed to the bank, rented a safe-deposit box and without a moment's notice started transferring the cigarette cases. He felt no relief until the last one was secure.

He went to the bank once a month to deposit two new cigarette cases. He always spent a considerable amount of time in the safe-deposit vault, enjoying the sight of the neatly stacked little cases. It was on one such occasion that an unexpected thought yet again shattered his moment of pleasure. It all started with an innocuous reflection as to whether the safe-deposit box he had rented was large enough to accommodate all his future nails.

Naturally, he could not know how many more nails there would be, but as a good mathematician it was not difficult to calculate that if he lived to the age of eighty-seven and a half years, the safe-deposit box would be filled to the top with cigarette cases. If he were to live longer than that he would have to rent either a larger box or an additional one if there were no larger boxes. This particular problem had a solution. But not the ultimate problem, one that hadn't crossed his mind before and suddenly struck with all its might. What would happen to the collection after his death?

He needed to prepare for this eventuality as soon as possible. True, there was no reason to worry, he was in excellent shape for his age, but disease is not the only cause of death. Various calamities are lying in wait, beyond our control. The worst thing possible would be for him to die a sudden death, before he was able to arrange for the permanent care of his collection. The safe-deposit box would be opened as part of his estate, necessarily divulging his secret.

This had to be prevented by all means. Yes, but how? Perhaps he could rent another safe-deposit box, not under his own name this time, but anonymously, so that his death would not result in its being opened? The box would still be opened at the end of the rental period. All right, then he would rent a box for a very long period. He wasn't quite sure how long that really long period should be—various durations crossed his mind, from one century to an entire millennium—but they told him at the bank that safe-deposit boxes were rented for a maximum of twenty-five years.

This certainly did not seem sufficient to him. He left the bank depressed, and this dismal mood never left him. The situation only worsened when he remembered another undesirable fact that had slipped by unnoticed. The nails on a corpse continue to grow for some time. He couldn't do anything about retrieving the lost fingernails of his childhood, so he simply had to make sure he got these. Should his collection be missing what might be its most important specimens? So, what should he do? He'd be dead and unable to cut his nails in the grave. Whom could he count on to cut them in his place?

Although this problem never left his mind, he couldn't find a solution—until one rainy afternoon when he least expected it. The solution struck him in a moment of profound enlightenment. It was magnificently elegant in its simplicity, like a mathematical formula. He felt like dancing with joy. He refrained, of course, as a man accustomed to well-mannered behavior, although no one would have seen him vent his exultation.

If death was the main obstacle standing in his way, then there was only one way to overcome it, once and for all. Mr. Prohaska firmly decided that he would never die.

Translated from the Serbian by Alice Copple Tošić.

6

Lost Illusions

Even though the telephone hadn't rung, the secretary picked up the receiver. Without a word, she listened to what was briefly said to her, then hung up the phone.

"You may go in." She motioned towards the padded door.

I got up and went into the office of the memory agency owner. The prevailing color was green. Plants of varying shapes and sizes were placed everywhere. The owner's large desk was covered with vegetation. When he stood up to greet me, holding a plastic sprayer, he looked like he'd just stepped out of a botanical garden.

"Hello. Please sit down."

I settled into a ponderous dark-brown leather armchair facing his desk. Tall oleanders in brass pots were placed on either side. When the owner sat down, all I could see was his head above the plants.

"So, you'd like to cash in your memory. Fine, fine. This is the first time you've put it up for sale, right?"

© Springer Nature Switzerland AG 2019
Z. Živković, *The Clay Writer*,
https://doi.org/10.1007/978-3-030-19753-7_6

Before entering his office I'd filled out a questionnaire that the secretary gave me. She'd entered my answers into the computer, so the owner could see them right away.

"Yes," I said.

"Many people find their first visit here quite a hardship. But please be assured that there is absolutely no reason to worry. First of all, the actual procedure of giving your memory is completely painless and not the least detrimental to your health. In addition, we don't remove your memory, we only make a copy of it. And finally, the buyer doesn't know whose memory he has purchased."

"It isn't easy, though. My memory is the most intimate part of me. It's like being without some part of my body."

"I agree it isn't easy if you look at it like an amputation or donating an organ for transplant. But it's not like that at all. Have you ever wondered what a memory actually is?"

He waited briefly, then continued since my reply was not forthcoming.

"Nothing real, tangible. Just an ordinary illusion whose loss is hardly felt. And why shouldn't a man lose some of his illusions if he can benefit by it, particularly when he's in trouble? Would you rather lose an organ?"

"No, I wouldn't," I had to admit.

"There, you see. And quite a profit can be made by selling illusions today. Some of our customers have really struck it rich. The market pays an excellent price, but is rather selective. I hope you have something interesting to offer us."

"I hope so, too."

"It would have been easy to find out if you'd let us scan your memory. Would you consider changing your mind?"

I shook my head briskly. "No, I wouldn't."

"I don't blame you. Few of our clients agree to it. People don't want to be an open book. That is something we understand and respect. Some things are kept even from the doctor. To tell you the truth, I myself wouldn't let anyone have unlimited access to my memory. A person has to keep some secrets to himself, right?"

"Indeed."

"The market, however, has the greatest demand for the very things we would most like to hide. That's also understandable. The urge to peep behind the curtain exists in all of us, whether we admit it or not. We are all voyeurs to a greater or lesser extent, and some people are ready to really loosen the purse strings to find pleasure in that passion."

I sighed. "Voyeurs won't be very attracted by what I have to offer."

"Ah, you never know. You can't imagine what all attracts the aficionados of other people's memories. Not long ago we sold the memory of a difficult childhood. You'd think that no one would be interested in it, yet it fetched an excellent price. Or, for example, the memory of days spent as a prisoner of war. Quite an unpleasant experience, but we found a rich buyer for that too. And what's there to say about a man who would give his eyeteeth for the memory of a childbirth. The more difficult and painful the memory, the more he is prepared to pay for it."

"There's nothing like that in my past." I smiled. "Certainly no childbirths."

He raised the sprayer and started to spray the plants on the desk in front of him. Several drops made it all the way to me.

"Of course. Perhaps there is something bizarre? Episodes with animals are in great demand right now. One customer received a pretty penny for the memory of eating a live snake. If it had been poisonous, she would have been set for life. The guy who sold his memory of falling off a horse didn't fare badly either. Too bad he was only bruised and not seriously injured. He would have gotten at least three times more. But you can't have everything. The highest price we ever received was for the memory of a night spent in a cage with a gorilla suffering from a toothache. We had to hold an auction."

"I don't have anything to offer with animals either."

"Very well. Then what do you have to offer?"

"I've read a lot of books."

He shook his head. "There's not much demand for that. Even if we find a buyer, you won't get hardly a thing. People are less and less interested in books. It doesn't help that they don't have to waste time reading anymore, since they can buy books already read. All they have to do is remember them. Such are the times, unfortunately."

"Unfortunately," I agreed.

"We might be able to raise the price if you've read a book that can't be found anymore and is enmeshed in a dangerous secret. The best would be a conspiracy of mammoth proportions that includes secret services, secret societies and the church, to be sure. There will always be fans for that."

I gave it some thought.

"There aren't any books like that among those I've read."

"What else do you have to offer?"

"I've been to a lot of celebrated classical music concerts."

The owner frowned. "There's not much profit in that either. A very narrow circle of people is interested in classical music, and they aren't very wealthy. We might attract one of the wealthier buyers if you have the memory of a concert that was involved in a scandal. An assassination attempt on the conductor, for example, or something like that."

"There weren't any scandals surrounding the concerts I attended."

"That's the downside of classical music. It's so stuffy and sterile. The very opposite of popular music where everything is bubbling with life. Live concerts have it all: fights, drugs, rape, weapons are even drawn. If you were a fan of that kind of music, you'd certainly have salable memories in abundance."

"Unfortunately, I'm not."

"Yes, unfortunately. What else do you have?" I could tell by his voice that he was starting to lose patience.

"I've visited famous museums and galleries."

The look he gave me was a mixture of reproach and pity. He raised the sprayer again, but didn't use it. He held it pointed at me.

"We won't get very far this way. You clearly don't know what's in demand on the memory market. It would be better if I asked you questions."

"All right."

"Is there any trauma from your childhood? Preferably with lots of abuse. Violence is always popular, particularly against children."

I shook my head. "There was no violence in my family."

"Too bad. Have you ever been in a traffic accident? Those with lots of casualties are highly prized. An airplane accident would be perfect."

"How could I be here now if I'd been in a plane crash?"

"Sometimes there are survivors. Their memories fetch a fabulous price."

"The only fall I remember was off a bicycle when I was seven and a half. I was covered in blood."

He seemed to be hesitating over whether to activate the sprayer.

"Have you witnessed an unusual event?"

"Unusual event?"

"Yes. The stranger the better. We got an excellent price for a chance bystander's memory of a three-story building that collapsed. Unprompted, without an earthquake. Thirteen dead. The witness of a suicide by jumping into an enormous vat full of honey also did well. The man who watched a tornado funnel suck up a train like it was a feather turned a good profit too. If it had been transporting people instead of sheep, he could have gotten whatever price he asked."

"Once I watched a heavy safe being lifted up to a fifth-floor window. They'd almost reached it when one of the cables snapped."

"Did it fall? Were there any casualties?"

"No. They somehow managed to get it inside."

"Tough luck. What about your sexual experience?"

"Excuse me?" I asked in amazement.

"Don't be surprised. Other people's sex life arouses voyeurs the most. Not just any, of course. No one's interested in ordinary lovemaking anymore. Perversity of any kind is all the rage. From incest to sodomy. You can't imagine the price that was paid for the memory of doing it with a giraffe. How about you?"

"Did I ever do it with a giraffe?"

"Not necessarily. Insects are currently in fashion. If you have any memory of intimate contact with termites, for example, or hornets, you'd be able to write your own check."

"My sex life is quite ordinary. No incest, giraffes or insects. And it's not for sale."

"As you wish. There's only one field left—crime. Traditionally it's the most lucrative."

"What kind of crime?"

"All of them sell superbly, particularly the most serious. Murder is highly valued. If the memory comes from the murderer himself, the sky's the limit. Can you offer something like that?"

"I haven't killed anyone."

The owner stood up and so did I.

"Then I'm afraid we can't be of any help at the moment." His tone spoke volumes of the fact that he was sorry he'd wasted his time with me. "If anything happens to enrich your memory, however, we will be glad to reconsider you."

He finally shot the water pistol. This time more than just a few drops reached me. If that hadn't happened, I would have simply left, equally unhappy with the time I'd lost. And for the humiliation I'd suffered. As it was, I had no choice.

I took out a real pistol and pulled the trigger without a second thought. The owner collapsed in silence onto the botanical garden.

I had to act quickly. Before the secretary collected her wits and the police came after me in hot pursuit, there was just enough time to go to another memory agency and leave a bit of first-class illusion there. If the sky was the limit, I'd get more than enough to spend a tranquil old age after I got out of prison. Filled with books, music and all kinds of art.

Translated from the Serbian by Alice Copple Tošić.

7

The First Loop

1

The surgeon had just dried his hands in a stream of hot air from the hand dryer next to the wash basin, pulled on his gloves and headed for the operating room, when a sudden recollection made him stop in front of the double glass door. Even though he was urgently awaited inside, the thought disconcerted him so much that he was rooted to the spot.

Those who knew him better would certainly have assumed that he'd remembered the incident he most wanted to forget. It was the only stain on his career. He'd left a pair of surgical tweezers inside a patient. There was no excuse for this oversight. What could he say in his defense? That he'd been captivated by her face and couldn't keep his eyes off her? The anesthesia had seemed to bestow an angelic quality on the beautiful young woman.

© Springer Nature Switzerland AG 2019
Z. Živković, *The Clay Writer*,
https://doi.org/10.1007/978-3-030-19753-7_7

Mentioning this enchantment as the cause of his distraction would only have aggravated his position.

But the surgeon was not thinking of this mishap just then, although it had happened in the room he was about to enter. Something else, considerably less unpleasant, had flashed across his mind, although there was no obvious reason for it.

He had gone to a colleague's wedding because he hadn't been able to get out of it. He didn't like weddings and even preferred funerals to them. Had anyone asked him why, he wouldn't have been able to explain. He found weddings repugnant, a perversity that embarrassed him. Indeed, what opinion could a doctor have of himself when he gave death priority over life?

In order to hide his bad mood, he'd acted out of character. A smile was stuck permanently on his face and he was annoyingly affable. As the wedding party gathered in front of the church, he struck up intimate conversations with people he hardly knew. He inquired after their health and offered advice even to those without any complaints. Since he was a reputable surgeon, everyone was grateful to receive his free counsel, even those in the pink of health.

He was relieved when they started to enter the church because this gave him a break from his feigned good humor. His face darkened, but he knew that as soon as they came out he would have to reassume a cheerful mask and keep it until late in the evening. Engrossed in somber thoughts, he failed to notice that the ceremony was delayed.

He realized that something was wrong from the commotion around him. Heads drew together as people whispered to each other. Shorter guests behind him craned their necks to get a better look at the altar where the wedding couple, best man and maid of honor were standing. Although he was right up front, it took a few moments before he detected the cause of the trouble.

There was no trace of the priest. The bride's agitation was clearly apparent even from her back. The bridegroom shrugged his shoulders helplessly and turned this way and that, but there was no one to give him an explanation. Who knew how long the uneasy tension would have lasted if the bride hadn't suddenly raised her veil and stamped her foot on the stone floor.

The blow of her thin heel resounded like an explosion in the echoing church. Everyone suddenly fell silent. She turned around brusquely and for some reason fixed her eyes on the surgeon. Words were not necessary. As though receiving a strict military order, he practically ran to the back of the church to see what was holding things up.

The surgeon knocked but received no reply. He waited briefly, then entered uninvited. A completely unexpected sight awaited him in the priest's little office. Most of the space was taken up by a massive pool table. The priest was standing motionless, bent all the way over it, holding a cue aimed at the white ball. All he had on below the waist was chequered long johns, black knee socks and slippers. It was not until the surgeon cleared his throat that the priest snapped out of his paralysis. As he quickly put on his pants, surplice and shoes, he tried to justify his behaviour.

He always played a bit of pool before a wedding ceremony. By himself and half-dressed. It was the best way to relax. This was the only ceremony that gave him the jitters. Hitting just two or three balls into the pockets was enough to calm him down. This time, however, as he swung the cue for the third time he suddenly remembered something and went stiff.

There was no time to satisfy the surgeon's curiosity. The priest was to blame for the wedding ceremony's late start. As soon as he had tied his shoelaces, they rushed out of the room. As they approached the altar, the priest's face turned penitent. The bride's stamping heel rang ominously in the church.

He mumbled something unintelligible in apology. The ceremony started at once and proceeded without a hitch. The bride's good mood returned as soon as she said "I do." On the way out of the church she was radiantly happy, as though there hadn't been any delay.

Had the surgeon known the priest better, no explanation would have been necessary. He would have assumed that the priest had recalled an event of twenty-six years ago, just after his appointment to this church. He was looking forward to the first wedding that was to install him officially in his duties. It had been scheduled before his arrival so he still hadn't had a chance to see the bride and groom.

When the wedding couple appeared before him he was thrown completely out of kilter. The face he glimpsed through the transparent veil took his breath away. He knew he shouldn't stare at the bride, but his eyes kept coming back to her. When the time came to start the ceremony, his memory failed him.

He stood there helplessly, mouth half-open, eyes fixed on the veil. Tension rose and his agony along with it, but he was unable to break the spell. When the bride, groom, best man and maid of honor started to look at each other in surprise, he finally managed to regain just enough control of himself to turn without a word and run to the priest's office.

Disaster was avoided owing to the fact that the recently retired former priest was in the church. He finished the ceremony that had barely started and then did his utmost to make allowances for his colleague. He ascribed the priest's disorientation to the jitters and lack of experience. When the wedding party left, he spent a long time consoling the young priest, telling him that something similar had happened to him as well at the beginning of his service.

The young priest felt better when he realized that no one had caught on to the cause of his embarrassment. He followed his colleague's advice about finding something to reduce his agitation before the ceremony. The retired priest, who used a pinball machine for the same purpose, saw nothing wrong with fulfilling the young man's wish to have a pool table in his office. He even used his influence to get a good price for a used table.

2

The memory of this distant embarrassment, however, was not what had now caused the priest to forget the bride, groom and wedding party awaiting him. He'd been held back by another memory that appeared out of the blue just as he was about to send the third ball into the pocket, then quickly get dressed and head toward the altar.

He'd remembered an incident at the theater that had almost turned into a scandal. The priest hadn't always been a theater buff. He would go occasionally to see a play when it seemed suitable to his calling. And then, suddenly, four-and-a-half years ago, he'd become a regular theatergoer. Sometimes he wouldn't miss a single performance the whole week long, even if the same play were given five times.

If anyone noticed the priest's sudden affinity for the theater, it aroused no suspicions. Why should it? Is there anything wrong with devotion to the theatrical arts stirring in a man of the cloth, even late in life? Had anyone taken a close look at what connected the plays he watched, they might have discovered that the priest's motives were not exactly above reproach. But who had any reason to undertake such an investigation?

Had there been a reason, the first thing to catch the eye was that the priest had warmed to the theater ever since a new young actress had started to play there. He watched only the plays in which she performed. He always sat in the same seat in the eleventh row, dressed in inconspicuous civvies. After every performance a bouquet of white roses awaited the actress in her dressing room, sent by a florist in the name of a fan who wanted to remain anonymous.

No investigation, however, would have ascertained what it was that bewitched the priest so much. The young actress was talented, but not exceptionally so. She was pretty too, although somewhat aloof. It might have been this detached beauty that attracted him, since priests are known for their unusual proclivities, but if someone could have penetrated the innermost corners of his mind, there where even he was unwilling to look, they would have discovered something else. The face hidden behind the veil was almost identical to that of the young actress. As though they were the same person. Such a similarity might be found, for example, in pictures of a mother and daughter taken when they were the same age.

Nothing indicated that something unusual would happen in the play. It was finely-tuned and had already been performed three times that week. At the beginning of the second act when the garden scene took place, the young actress was alone on the stage with an actor who was still cast in the role of a Don Juan even though he'd been dyeing his hair for years and wore a corset to fight his excess weight.

At his fiery declaration, "You must be mine," accompanied by an attempt to kiss her, she was supposed to push him away, slap him lightly and shout "What's come over you?" But she did none of that. She stood there without moving, staring over his shoulder into the audience as though struck dumb by something she saw there.

Those who hadn't seen the play before found nothing strange at first. The young woman was supposed to reject the courtship of her aggressive seducer, but this might be an unexpected turn that was characteristic of such plays. Indeed, he was holding her rather awkwardly, as though equally surprised by the lack of resistance. The priest, however, who knew the play perfectly, realized at once that something unusual was going on.

As the seconds passed tensely and the actress just stood there thunderstruck, the audience started to fidget. The priest felt panic creep over him, as though he himself were on the stage. At first he thought the young woman had forgotten her lines, although this had never happened before. Since he already knew most of her role by heart, he was tempted to call out the line to her from the gloom, but before he could do so, the prompter beat him to it and practically shouted, "What's come over you?"

The shout caused an even greater stir in the audience. Two low whistles were heard. It was certain that general discontent would be quick to follow, with the inevitable suspension of the play. Had the priest thought it over, he might have hesitated. Unwarranted public displays were certainly not suitable to his position and reputation. But now he had no choice.

He jumped up from his seat and briskly applauded. The audience turned their eyes from the stage to him. When they recognized him in the gloom, they hesitated just a moment and then joined his applause. Is there any better example to follow than that of a priest? If he doesn't know what should be done, who does?

As though the thundering sound had snapped her out of her paralysis, the young actress returned to her role more spiritedly than necessary. With the shrill cry, "What's come over you?" she slapped the actor and pushed him so violently that he, who was only holding her lightly, lost his balance and fell flat on his back with his long legs flying in the air. This brought an outburst of laughter that instantly erased the theatergoers' peevishness over the hitch of a moment before.

The play continued seamlessly with even greater inspiration than usual and in the end the actors were brought back on stage for seven curtain calls. For days afterwards rumors were spread about what had come over the young actress. For some mysterious reason she refused to offer any explanation. The theater's management did not insist on getting one owing to the favorable outcome.

The only apology the young woman gave was to her older colleague who didn't begrudge her very much for disgracing him since he'd turned the incident to his advantage. He soon stopped playing suitors and seducers, and turned to comic roles full of gags where he managed quite well and no longer had to dye his hair and wear a corset.

Most people supported the hypothesis that the empty third seat in the right front row was to blame for everything. Those sitting nearby remembered that an extremely handsome young man no one had seen before had been occupying that seat during the first act. Several of them claimed they'd seen the young actress glance towards him frequently, always with a fleeting smile, even when the role did not occasion it.

Why the young man did not return to the auditorium after the intermission remained a mystery. When the young woman noticed he was gone she'd turned completely numb. Was this to be held against her? Everyone knows how hard it is when your loved one spurns you, and this had been done in front of so many eyewitnesses. Everyone sympathized with her grief, which only increased her popularity.

3

The rumors went all the way to the young actress. She did not deny them, however, because this was not to her advantage. She shrewdly kept her mouth shut even though she knew there wasn't a grain of truth to any of it. First of all, even if she'd wanted to see someone in the audience, in the front row or any other, this was impossible because the stage lights practically blinded her. In addition, she wasn't in love with the handsome young man because she didn't even know who he was.

Finally, if she started to deny the story she would have to explain what had made her almost interrupt the performance, and this was something she certainly wanted to avoid. Among other things, there was nothing romantic about the real reason. Without that ingredient she would lose the public's sympathy and the management's regard.

What had completely thrown her out of the role she was playing was a memory that suddenly crossed her mind. She remembered a fire that had engulfed a two-story residential building in her neighborhood. She'd been nine-and-a-half at the time. Never before or after would she directly experience the horrors of an uncontrolled blaze. Standing at a safe distance, she watched the flames rise from the basement where something had caught fire. Water streaming from the firefighters' hoses seemed to have no effect.

Shouts were heard from all around when a window in the attic opened and a terrified old woman appeared. She was screaming for help, waving her arms. A ladder quickly sprang up from one of the fire trucks. Before it even reached the attic, a fully outfitted, heavyset firefighter grabbed hold of a rung.

He took hold of the woman around the waist. Nothing happened for a few moments. Her shaking head indicated that she was too afraid to go down. The firefighter had to take off his mask so she could hear him.

Everyone breathed a sigh of relief when she finally put her arms around his neck. He lifted her with ease and started down the ladder as the onlookers cheered. But everyone fell silent when he stopped unexpectedly about halfway down the ladder. His helmet and her gray head turned towards the window in the attic that was now empty. The firefighter took off his mask once again to calm her down as she held on with one hand and pointed up with the other.

He spent a good 2 min reassuring the woman before they started down again. When they reached the roof of the truck, the firefighter's colleagues took hold of her and he started up the ladder again. Even though the hoses were turned on full blast, the fire had devoured the first floor in the meantime and fiery tongues were flicking towards the second. But this did not deter the courageous firefighter.

He hastened inside when he reached the window and spent only a few moments there, although it seemed much longer to the crowd. When he reappeared he was carrying a cage with a small white parrot fluttering about in distress. Applause filled the air.

The firefighter had just straddled the window when he saw the old woman's arms waving to him from the ground. He couldn't make out what she was shouting in distress, but it seemed this was not even necessary. He hesitated briefly about what to do with the cage, then finally let it fall into the outstretched canvas out at the bottom of the ladder. Before he went back into the room he made sure that the parrot had survived the fall, even though the worn-out cage had broken to pieces.

This time it was not merely an impression. The firefighter was gone for a long time. During that time the fire spread to the second floor. Now the hoses were focused on the narrow space around the ladder to keep the fire at bay, but this would clearly not work for very long. A terrible roar had begun inside.

The commander of the fire brigade knew he had no choice. His hand was already raised to signal the truck to lower the ladder and move back when the firefighter appeared in a cloud of smoke pouring out of the attic window. Under his arm was a small chest of valuables.

Elated cheering mixed with shouts urging him to hurry. Just as he started to descend the ladder again the smoke above him turned red and flames darted out of the window. Luckily he was beyond their reach, but there was no time to lose. He had to get down as quickly as possible. The truck couldn't move while he was on the ladder.

As an experienced firefighter, he was certainly aware of this, but even so he stopped at approximately the same place as he had the first time he went down. When it became clear that this was not just a brief stop, all hell broke loose. The fire was now blazing from all the openings on the building and had already broken through the roof.

The other firefighters shouted at him to continue, but he just stood there motionless on the same rung. He must have been overcome by the heat and smoke in spite of the gas mask and protective suit. The hoses turned on him to cool him off and bring him back to his senses. This was all they could do. No one dared go up to him because it was already too dangerous.

As he stood there like a statue, the crowd was struck with horror. The building was about to collapse and he was sure to die. Many turned their heads away. The little girl, however, continued to watch. And not only that.

She started to sing. Quite softly, so that in the surrounding noise she couldn't even hear herself. Had anyone been watching they would have thought she was mouthing the words. But no one paid any attention to the little girl who, in any case, had no business to be there.

It must have been a coincidence. The firefighter on the ladder was the last person who could have heard her little tune. Nevertheless, as soon as she started, he suddenly came to his senses. Instead of climbing, he slid down in a flash. The little girl didn't stop until he was safely on the ground and the truck had withdrawn. The moment the inaudible song ended, the building collapsed with a tremendous crash and burst of flames.

The fire was finally put out an hour-and-a-half later, but the little girl left as soon as the firefighter was saved. After the men returned to the fire station, no one asked why he'd stopped on the ladder. They were all convinced they knew the answer. The glowing heat and smoke hadn't dazed him. The little chest was to blame.

The object the fireman went back to retrieve from the attic must have reminded him of a distant event that he'd mentioned only once to his colleagues in an unprecedented state of drunkenness at a fireman's ball and later, when he sobered up, refused to talk about again.

Before he became a firefighter he'd worked for over four years as a lighthouse keeper on a small island quite distant from land. One gray autumn morning he had a surprise waiting for him on the deserted rocky coast—a shipwrecked boat with no one inside. The ocean current must have brought it from far away.

Inside the boat was a wooden chest with metal studs. It measured about one meter by half a meter and reached up to his knees. A gold chain with an oval locket was attached to the large padlock. When he removed the chain, he noticed that the locket opened. Inside was a black and white picture of the most beautiful young woman he had ever seen. He couldn't tear his eyes away for a long time.

Finally he returned to the lighthouse and brought back his toolbox. He knew that he wasn't allowed to do anything on his own. The rules required that he radio the lighthouse management and wait for a maritime inspector, but the young woman's face seemed to have completely confused him. He simply had to open the chest, which he'd already ascertained was quite heavy. There was no way he could bring it to shore by himself.

It took quite a bit of effort before he finally forced the padlock. Kneeling next to the chest, he raised the lid halfway. All he did was stare for some time, oblivious to the rain that had started to drizzle. Then he closed the lid slowly and rummaged briefly through his toolbox until he found a new padlock. He put it in place of the broken one and attached the chain to it.

Then he brought a motor boat from the lighthouse harbor, tied a rope to the shipwrecked boat and headed out to open sea. When he thought he was far enough from the island, he stopped. Taking an axe from the motor boat, he got into the wrecked ship and started breaking its hull without a second thought. When water started pouring in, he returned to his boat and untied the rope, then watched until the boat with the chest went under. On regaining the lighthouse, he informed his superiors that he was resigning. He would no longer do the job of a lighthouse keeper.

The firefighter's colleagues did everything they could to find out what he'd seen in the chest but he, in spite of his drunken state, had kept the secret to himself. Now that unfinished story had come in handy. He didn't have to explain what had come over him during his second descent from the attic with its near-tragic end.

4

What had come over him was a sudden flashback that had nothing to do with the mysterious chest. Later when he gave it more thought, he couldn't figure out what it was that had brought forth that distant memory just then, at such a badly chosen moment.

He'd been very interested in athletics as a young man. He'd never tried his own hand at it, even though he had the build of a sportsman, but regularly attended competitions. He was particularly attracted to women's throwing events. Not that there was anything perverse about it. He admired the power and skill of the throwers. In addition, he felt that the spectators wrongfully neglected them as not looking feminine enough.

This was confirmed at the event that had flashed back to him out of the blue on the ladder. The spectators' attention was riveted on the slender, long-legged female high jumpers and hardly anyone was watching the part of the field where shots were being put, even though it was just as exciting.

It was the end of the last series of puts. Only one contestant was left. She was in second place and this was her chance to come in first. The future lighthouse keeper had been rooting for her from the beginning, although he couldn't explain why. Her stature was no different from her opponents'. All that set her apart was her wavy red hair.

She entered the putting circle. In her previous five attempts she had put the shot immediately, but now for some reason she hesitated. She just stood there with her back to the putting circle, looking somewhere to the side. At first he thought she was trying her best to concentrate. He was angry at the spectators cheering for the high jumpers because they were distracting her.

Moments passed and the shot putter didn't move. When the small digital countdown next to the circle indicated she had only seven seconds left for her last put, her sole supporter did something that was quite out of character for someone as reserved as he was.

He jumped up from his seat and shouted, "Put it!" But his cry was drowned out by thunderous applause for the woman who had just bested the highest jump. It was not clear whether the putter heard him or snapped out of her torpor owing to this outburst of joy in the bleachers.

In any case, she began her circular start at once. When the shot flew out of her left hand, the countdown had reached the number two. The distance she put the shot was not immediately clear. This, however, didn't seem to interest anyone but the other putters and one spectator.

When it was announced that she had put the shot three centimeters farther than the leading contestant, he jumped up again and started to clap, paying no attention to the dubious looks of the spectators around him. After he sat down, he wondered what it was that had inhibited the red-headed young woman to the point of almost failing to put the shot. He pondered a moment, but was unable to detect any reason. In any case, whatever it was, it no longer mattered now that she'd won.

Had he been one of those who knew the shot putter better, he would have concluded that her hesitation was connected to the memory of a dramatic event from the beginning of her career in athletics. At that time she threw the javelin instead of putting the shot, and her first competition almost had a fateful end.

Then as now she had one throw left. She'd gone onto the run-up area and had already started to run, when something on the right caught her eye. She continued with her head turned halfway until she threw the javelin. As soon as it flew out of her hand, she realized the inexorable.

The sharp double-bladed spear had gone too far to the side. She shouted while the javelin was still going up. Her shout reached many ears, but not those of the long jumper who, suspecting nothing, was warming up next to the track at the other end of the stadium.

At first it seemed that he'd been hit in the stomach. The terrified young woman covered her mouth with her hands and collapsed in a heap at the end of the run-up area. When they brought her around, they first cheered her with the news that the worst had been avoided. The javelin had pierced his hip. He wouldn't be able to jump anymore but at least his life was not in danger.

The young woman at first decided to drop athletics too, but the young man she had injured talked her out of it. He told her she had to continue for both of them. She agreed, but changed disciplines. Owing to her build she would still have to be a thrower. She chose the shot because she thought it was the least dangerous for others.

For a while they tried to find out what had made her look to the side while she'd been running with the javelin. Probably owing to the shock she'd experienced, she had absolutely no recollection of those moments. This gave rise to rumors. It was said that she'd caught sight of a handsome sprinter who was lying on the grass limbering up. He was by no means the only good-looking athlete, but the thrower felt that his wavy red hair made him unique.

This time no one asked her why she almost failed to put her last shot. Indeed, except for the one and only supporter, only the other putters were aware of her hesitation. Those who knew about the injured long jumper were convinced she'd been thinking about that. The other women saw the whole thing as a tactical maneuver that they would have to use as well.

5

The young woman was glad she didn't have to explain herself. She surely would have disappointed many people if she'd told them what really happened when she entered the shot putting circle. It had not been any sort of tactical subterfuge. Something had crossed her mind, but not the unfortunate javelin throw. She'd remembered another far more innocuous incident in which the long jumper also had a minor role.

When he recovered from his injuries, he invited her out to dinner. She couldn't refuse, of course, although she would have under other circumstances. She had a feeling of guilt about the young man, but nothing else. He wasn't her type. If he decided to try anything, she would have to let him know, in spite of everything.

Luckily, he had no such intentions. They spent the evening making cheerful small talk. Although they spent most of the time talking about athletics, neither one mentioned the unpleasant incident that had brought them together. She soon relaxed and started to enjoy his company, deciding that it would be nice for them to become friends, since anything else was out of the question.

The only small shadow cast that evening came during dessert. An older couple was sitting at the table next to theirs. He was tall and thin, completely gray, but with a thick crop of hair. His comportment was stiff and stern. He was silent most of the time. She was short and round, all in pink. Her matching hat had a wide brim and several brightly colored feathers. She never closed her mouth.

There was no indication that something might go wrong. The liveried waiter went up to take their order. He waited patiently next to the table as the new guests examined the unwieldy menu inside its dark-brown leather cover. Either the abundant selection or their discrimination resulted in a protracted wait.

The lady was the first to speak. She asked for an explanation of several items on the menu. The waiter did not reply. He just looked at her, smiling. She repeated her question, but again there was no answer. Then she turned to her husband who was still engrossed in the menu. He raised his head and addressed the waiter himself. The man continued to stand there without speaking, leaning forward a little, holding a pad in one hand and a pen in the other. The smile never left his face.

After a brief silence, the woman repeated her question in a louder voice. But it seemed to be directed at a statue. Perplexed by the waiter's demeanor, the couple looked around for his colleagues. Right then, however, none of the other staff were in the restaurant's main dining room.

The young woman couldn't imagine what had come over the waiter. When he'd served them, everything had seemed perfectly fine. He'd been very obliging and pleasant. She had no reason to interfere, but as the tension mounted with no relief in sight, she felt more and more uncomfortable, as though personally involved in the problem at the next table.

She looked at the long jumper. He just shrugged his shoulders, clearly at a loss. She felt a knot growing in her stomach, just like before a decisive throw on the athletic field. She had to do something to make it go away. Hesitating just a moment, she reached for her unused wine glass, picked it up and dropped it with a swing.

The explosion of shattering glass echoed in the hush of the restaurant. Every single guest flinched. Some even jumped up. The maître d' and the other waiters swarmed out of the kitchen. Even the head chef made an appearance. But most important of all, the strangely statue-like waiter came back to his senses.

He mumbled a few words of apology and hastened to clean up the broken glass. Realizing what had happened, the maître d' quickly took the waiter's place at the elderly couple's table. His cordiality soon removed their unease and in no time at all nothing in the restaurant indicated that anything unusual had happened.

No one held it against the waiter. On the contrary, they were all reassuring and full of understanding, convinced they knew what had caused the incident. The feathered hat was to blame, of course. It had reminded him of something that happened at that same table. Even though more than five years and three months had passed since then, he still hadn't forgotten the trauma.

The only thing that disrupted the guest's widow's weeds was a yellow hat with ostrich feathers. She was already well along in years and yet had a youthful appearance. She was without an escort and yet not alone. She had brought a cage, holding it by the ring on the domed top.

After she sat down, she took the black cover off the cage. The waiter was on his way to her table and stopped in mid-step. Never before had he seen such a lovely creature. He knew nothing about birds so he didn't know what it was called, but did that matter? Mesmerized, he stared at the magnificent plumage all ablaze, shimmering in every color of the rainbow.

The woman had to clear her throat to bring the waiter to his senses. It took considerable effort for him to tear his eyes away from the cage. He handed her the menu but she waved it away dismissively. She turned towards the bird and addressed it in a low voice full of guttural vowels that sounded like cooing.

The bird replied with a warble that sent shudders down the waiter's spine and filled his ears with the sound of heavenly choirs. When the guest addressed him again, he only half-glanced at her and wrote down the order in a daze. On his way to the kitchen he looked back several times.

It was not until he returned, carrying a roast pigeon in wild strawberry sauce, that he wondered at the woman's unusual choice. Indeed, eating a bird in the company of another bird did not seem quite proper. But of course, it was not for him to judge the guests' preferences.

He set the plate of roast pigeon before the woman, poured her a glass of white wine and wished her a pleasant meal. This time he did not look back as he walked away. When he reached the place he stood while waiting to serve the guests, he turned around again, looked towards the table with the cage—and was horrified.

He had misunderstood. The dish was not intended for the woman but the bird. The plate was inside the cage. The creature with heavenly plumage and a divine song was tearing off pigeon meat with its beak and gobbling it voraciously. The woman watched it with a smile as she sipped her wine.

The waiter felt nauseous. Putting both hands over his mouth, he ran to the men's room and spent a good 10 min there, first with his head over the toilet and then splashing his face over the sink. It took a little while longer to muster the courage to go back to the restaurant's main dining room.

He looked reluctantly towards the place where the beauty had defiled herself so foully, fearing a new attack of nausea, but there was no cause for concern. The woman with the cage had left. On the table was a plate full of tiny bones and a half-drunk glass of wine.

The waiter decided at first to leave the profession, even though he had talent that promised a successful career. It took the restaurant owner a long time to make him change his mind. It was only when the owner gave him a raise and promised to ban birds from the restaurant that he accepted.

6

The waiter had no reason to disillusion his colleagues and the maître d'. Let them think the old trauma was behind the whole thing. They wouldn't have had much understanding for his unseemly conduct if they knew what had really caused it. The memory that resurged as he was waiting for the guests to make up their minds was not stirred by the feathers on the pink hat because3   they   weren't ostrich feathers. He never did figure out what had called forth that event of six years and seven months ago which had lain dormant for so long.

An undertaker friend of his had asked him to the Funeral Association's annual costume ball. He reluctantly agreed to go. He didn't like this type of party and he didn't know how to act in the company of morticians. His friend assured him that it was just a costume ball like any other and he had no reason to worry. He would see, in effect, that undertakers were more inclined to enjoy a bit of fun than people with far cheerier professions.

He vacillated a long time in the costume supply shop until he finally chose a Frosty the Snowman mask. Even though the mask was more of a caricature, it somehow seemed the most appropriate.

The costume ball was in full swing: blaring music, flowing drinks, rafters echoing with laughter. Everyone hid behind their masks and this added to the dissolute, loose atmosphere. Among so many grotesque faces, Frosty the Snowman seemed quite artless, until the highpoint of the party when the time came for the undertakers' reel.

Everyone danced. More than one hundred fifty undertakers and guests surrendered completely to the whirling rhythm. Two turns were made, hands on the hips of one's partner, and then the couples split up and new ones formed. The room seemed filled with a multitude of whirling, volatile circles.

Since the waiter wasn't a good dancer, he would rather have sat it out, but that was impossible. Fortunately, he quickly mastered the simple steps and then the dizzying rapture seized him too. Squealing and whooping masks changed before him without letup.

He had just put his hands on the hips below a fiendish witch mask that certainly didn't match the luxuriant dark wavy hair and slender build, when his new partner stopped dead in her tracks. This caused a chain reaction, such as when one of many interconnected gears suddenly stops. The harmonious atmosphere reigning until then collapsed like a house of cards. The orchestra fell silent because it had lost its purpose.

The waiter stared in confusion at the slits in the witch mask where chestnut eyes stared at him emptily. At the same time, he felt the reproachful glances of the other dancers shoot straight at him in the muffled silence. They clearly believed that his clumsiness had caused the holdup.

Panic was already coursing through his body when he realized what he had to do. He ripped off the Frosty the Snowman mask. Nothing moved for a few moments and then the young woman's hands resting limply on his hips suddenly held him tight.

He hoped he had properly interpreted the sign and led her into the whirling dance again. Only two circles were needed for all the gears in the room to start working. Even before the music started up again he had a new mask in front of him. He didn't put his own mask back on. The undertakers' reel continued triumphantly and everyone forgot the brief interruption.

In the general tumult at the end when the masks were removed, he was unable to find the face of the young woman with the wavy hair and chestnut eyes. On the way back from the costume party his friend explained what had undoubtedly caused the dance to break off. It was the Frosty the Snowman mask, of course, and an incident that had happened the summer before.

The young woman, whom everyone considered to be the prettiest member of the Funeral Association, had been in a bank when there was an attempted robbery. She was standing in line in front of the counter when a shot rang out behind her. She turned around in alarm to see a heavyset man wearing a Frosty the Snowman mask, holding a gun. Speaking calmly, as though nothing unusual was going on, he ordered the employees to raise their hands and the customers to lie on the floor, then disarmed the guard who hadn't had time to react.

Just as he went up to the counter and handed over a bag to be filled with money, the alarm went off. Metal shutters dropped over the windows the same moment. The robber ordered the employees to continue as though nothing had happened. Then he took the bagful of money, went to an armchair in the corner and sat down.

In less than 3 min the wailing of a police siren came from outside. A telephone line to the robber was soon set up. Still speaking calmly, he ordered the police to send him a helicopter in 20 min so he could get away with the loot. He threatened to start killing the hostages he was holding in the bank if they didn't meet his demands.

When the time was up and he was asked to be patient since they were having trouble finding him a helicopter, he simply hung up. His eyes slid over the customers on the floor and then he motioned with his gun for the young female undertaker to get up. An older man lying next to her tried to protest, but stopped as soon as the barrel was pointed at his head.

He took the young woman to a back room. Everyone waited in horror for the ominous shot, but nothing was heard. Ten minutes later the customers started getting up slowly, and the more courageous employees lowered their hands. They looked at each other in bewilderment.

At the sound of the back door opening, they quickly returned to their former positions. The robber came out of the back room. He was no longer wearing the Frosty the Snowman mask and his gun was gone. A few moments later the young woman appeared. One hand held the pistol barrel gingerly with two fingers and the other held the mask.

The telephone rang that same moment. The police announced that the helicopter was on its way. The robber replied that it was no longer necessary. He had decided to surrender. He hung up the phone and returned to the armchair next to the bag of money where he waited quietly for them to arrest him.

The police tried to find out what had happened in the back room. The young woman, however, refused to talk, even when threatened with being accused as an accessory. They couldn't get the robber to loosen his tongue either. Not even the promise of a lighter sentence was any help.

7

None of the pretty undertaker's colleagues asked why she'd interrupted the last dance. They were all convinced they knew the reason. But even if they'd asked, there would have been no reply. The unusual incident in the circus that had suddenly surfaced was no one else's concern. She couldn't fathom what had summoned that memory in the middle of the whirling, but it certainly hadn't been Frosty the Snowman.

It was just after her thirteenth birthday. Two of her girlfriends had talked her into going to the circus that had just come to town. She didn't like circuses, particularly not the acts with trained animals. She was horrified at the thought of the torture they went through just to entertain the crowd.

Fortunately, this circus did not have many trained animals. The show was already well along and there had only been a little monkey that seemed to be thoroughly enjoying itself. Just when she'd begun to hope that was it, a lion taming act appeared at the very end.

It was immediately clear that the three large beasts, a male and two females, were quite agitated. The tamer had to crack his whip constantly and raise a chair to get them to obey his commands. The lions thrashed their paws menacingly as the tent reverberated with angry roars.

The high point of the act was when the tamer put his head into the male lion's open mouth. He seemed reluctant, then signaled the audience to be quiet. Silence reigned. He put down the chair, laid the whip on it and cautiously headed towards the lion.

As he drew closer, the future undertaker was suddenly struck by the great cat's beauty. Everything about it seemed harmonious and full of raw energy. Even its roar that had made her shudder a moment before now seemed almost melodious.

The tamer stood stock-still for a moment in front of the lion. Then he slowly raised his hands and opened its jaw. He looked the animal straight in the eye for a few moments, then put his head between the pointed teeth.

The admiring audience watched with bated breath as the tension quickly rose. It seemed they could hardly wait for the act to end so they could thunderously applaud. But the seconds drew out and nothing happened. The tamer's head did not come out of the lion's mouth.

When it became clear that something was wrong, the crowd began to fidget. Was the lion preventing the tamer from removing his head? The man made no movement that would indicate he was in trouble, but the animal was clearly struggling to keep its jaws open, as though wanting to close its mouth as soon as possible.

While many in the audience put their hands over their eyes, horrified at what seemed imminent, the girl suddenly felt a thrill such as she had never experienced before. It was as if the tamer's head was inside her own mouth. She started to open and close her jaws.

She didn't snap out of this peculiar trance until the chattering sound caused one of her young womanfriends to look at her strangely. She clenched her jaw firmly shut in embarrassment. That same moment, to everyone's relief, the tamer finally took his head out of the lion's mouth.

While rounds of applause still filled the tent, the young woman stood up and left without a word. She never went to a circus again. When she got home, she firmly resolved to be an undertaker when she grew up. She never told anyone the reason for this decision.

Unlike the audience, the circus staff took the end of the lion tamer's act in stride. It was not unusual for him to keep his head in the lion's mouth for quite some time. That meant that he was thinking of a tragic event from his youth.

He had the adventurous spirit that went hand in hand with becoming a lion tamer and often set out to explore uncharted regions. Once he chanced to meet a young woman with a similar penchant. He didn't hesitate a moment to accept her invitation to join in the search for a mysterious underground city in the heart of the jungle.

With the help of an ancient map, they proceeded through the wilds, overcoming dangerous obstacles along the way. When they finally reached their destination at the close of the ninth day on the road, an amazing sight

awaited them. The setting sun illuminated a rocky elevation carved in the shape of a human skull.

In place of the mouth was a gaping semicircular opening into a cave. The only way to enter was to get on one's
hands and knees. The young woman was all set to go right
in, but he managed to talk her out of it. Night was about
to fall and they were quite tired. It would be better to
sleep outside and start exploring in the morning.

When he awoke, the young woman was not next to
him. He realized at once what had happened. He rushed
to the entrance, but had a surprise in store. Inexplicably,
the opening had shrunk. He could no longer go all the
way inside; only his head would fit.

Filled with dark foreboding, he stuck his head through
the opening. He assumed he wouldn't see anything, but
never guessed the reason: not because of the darkness but
just the opposite—because of the dazzling light. It was as
if the sun itself had moved into the cave. He had to squint
to prevent himself being blinded.

He heard the young woman's terrified voice from down
in the depths. She begged him to leave at once. He, of
course, would never have left her, but that's when he felt
the stone mouth start to close around his head. Terror-
stricken, he pulled it out at the last moment before the
opening in the skull disappeared for good.

The only way to get inside was with dynamite, but
he hadn't brought any with him. Driven by despair, he
reached civilization in only six days. He got the equipment
he needed and rushed back, but when he got there the
skull-shaped elevation was nowhere to be seen.

He wandered frantically through the nearby jungle for
days, hoping he'd gone astray without the map that had
stayed with the young woman. But there wasn't a trace of
the entrance into the underground world of light. Finally,
totally crushed, he had to give up.

8

The lion tamer was glad that no explanation was due to the circus staff as to why he'd hesitated from taking his head out of the lion's mouth. As an honest man he didn't want to lie, which is what he would have had to do to avoid even greater trouble. It was better this way. Let them believe that he'd remembered the incident in the jungle. They'd all shown consideration for that trauma, but it would certainly be lacking if they knew what thought had imperiled the act and put his own life in danger.

He had suddenly remembered a distant auction he'd attended more out of curiosity than to buy anything. The small town where he'd settled for a while after retiring from his life as an adventurer held auctions every Saturday morning in the only movie theater in town.

The locals usually brought small household items to sell: vases, candlesticks, inkpots, bookends, old medals and coins, porcelain figurines, picture frames, sets of silverware, wall clocks and watches. Nice little things could be bought for a trifle.

Nothing indicated that anything unusual would happen at the auction. A pipe-cleaning set from the last century, two gramophone records of operatic arias and a teapot that could only be used as a decoration had all been sold. Their brisk sale was certainly facilitated by the smooth tongue of the experienced auctioneer, a retired lady doctor with salt-and-pepper hair and a large mole on her left cheek.

Her assistant lifted the next item on the list for that Saturday. It was a harmonica in a little, worn-out cardboard box. He handed it to the closest person in the front row. The custom was to give the auction attendees a chance to see the offered items up close. As it went from hand to hand, the auctioneer would sing its praises.

The harmonica had just reached the future lion tamer when he realized that something was wrong. He looked around in confusion and noted that everyone's eyes were turned toward the auctioneer. Instead of a stream of words bubbling out of her mouth, she was as silent as a stone. Her eyes were staring blankly somewhere above the attendees' heads.

The former adventurer was in a bind. He didn't know what to do with the little box. The man on his left didn't seem interested in taking it and there was no sense in handing it back to the woman on his right who had given it to him. In the tense silence that settled over the movie theater, he wavered briefly over what to do. Then, without knowing what brought him to it, he took out the little instrument and started to play.

Had the circumstances been normal, everyone would have considered this quite uncouth. But now the aversion was missing. Heads slowly turned towards him. Faces were smiling. A few moments later there was spontaneous applause. The lion tamer stopped playing and bowed in bewilderment.

The auctioneer's voice came to life that same moment. As though waking from a dream, she started animatedly to highlight the qualities of the harmonica. The lion tamer's neighbor took it impatiently, but kept it only briefly since the other auction-goers could barely wait to see it up close.

The excited bidding that soon followed led to a dizzying price for the little instrument. It was bought by the fat owner of the butcher shop who doubled the pharmacist's last bid. The former adventurer only took part in the bidding briefly and then withdrew. He realized that something unusual was going on, but he didn't have a clue what it was.

Later that day in the bar that was the center of the small town's social life, he heard the story of what had struck the auctioneer dumb when the harmonica went on sale. It was the memory of an incident from her youth.

Just like every other Sunday morning during the summer, she had been walking with a girlfriend in the nearby rolling hills. They always went the same way, covering eleven-and-a-half kilometers through the picturesque countryside. When they reached about halfway, they would stop to rest for a quarter of an hour on a bench made of roughly hewn wood on the edge of the forest.

That morning they could already see from a distance that someone was sitting there. At first they thought it was one of the locals, but when they got a bit closer it turned out to be a stranger. Her girlfriend proposed that they head back, but the future auctioneer, who was studying medicine at the time, convinced her that they had no reason to worry. What could happen to them?

As they drew closer, the features of the man on the bench became more distinguishable. Although neither one of them spoke, they both thought the same thing. Never before had they seen such a handsome young man. They had a terrible time keeping their eyes off him in spite of the rudeness of such staring.

When they were some fifteen paces from the bench, the young man reached for the inside pocket of his jacket and took out a harmonica. As though oblivious to their arrival, gazing somewhere off in the distance, he put the little instrument to his lips and started to play. The young women stopped and looked at each other in amazement.

The melody was simple, but seemed to have something intoxicating about it. It didn't have the same effect on both young women. Her girlfriend became nervous and wanted to leave again immediately, while the future auctioneer was enchanted.

Not long after the young man started to play, he got up from the bench, turned around and headed into the forest.

The dense underbrush and foliage soon swallowed him up. He didn't seem too far away, though, since the pleasing music reached them clearly on the other side of the opaque curtain of vegetation.

The young women looked at each other again and then, without a word of explanation, the medical student headed into the forest. The auctioneer's girlfriend watched in disbelief as she disappeared at the same place as the young man and shouted in alarm for her to return, but all that came back from the forest was the sound of the harmonica.

She turned this way and that in confusion for a while, not knowing what to do. She didn't have the courage to go into the forest too. Finally she headed back to the small town, almost at a run. Two hours and ten minutes later she was back at the bench, this time with two policemen.

When no one replied to her calls, the policemen headed into the forest. They came back 15 min later empty-handed. An extensive search was launched that same afternoon. Much of the countryside was explored, but there was no trace of the young woman and the young man.

The search was suspended because of the dark and then continued the next day with specially trained dogs, again with no results. When the search party returned at the end of the next day with the job undone, it was clear that they would have to give up. The earth seemed to have swallowed up the people they were looking for.

The young woman had already been given up for lost, when she suddenly appeared in town four days after her disappearance in the forest. There was no sign that anything was wrong with her. She seemed serene, as though just returning from her customary walk.

They showered her with questions, wanting to find out what had happened. But she stubbornly refused to divulge anything, even to the police who called her in for an interview. Since she hadn't broken any law by disappearing, they had to reconcile themselves to her silence.

This, however, gave rise to various rumors. They even reached her ears, but she just laughed everything off. The gossip gained momentum when she continued to take her Sunday walk, no longer accompanied by her girlfriend.

Those who were most inquisitive started to follow her at a distance. They watched her enter the thicket behind the bench, but no one had the courage to go in after her. Some who went up closer swore that they heard the sound of a harmonica coming from the underbrush.

The young woman would stay in the forest for two or three hours, and then return to town beaming with joy. This went on until the beginning of fall when she went back to the city and her medical studies. The next summer she went home again for vacation. She continued taking walks, but no longer towards the bench on the edge of the forest.

9

When it came time for the harmonica, the auctioneer had indeed remembered that long-past summer, but this is not why she'd been lost in thought; rather it was because of another more innocent memory that flashed out of the blue right afterwards.

As a young intern, she'd gained experience assisting at operations. She was on duty when they started bringing in people who had been injured in the collision of two subway trains. All the surgeons who were not on duty were quickly summoned. The operating rooms were in a state of emergency.

On the table in front of her was a patient with serious internal injuries. He had already bled quite a bit and had to be operated on at once. The surgeon, however, had yet to arrive and she, who was insufficiently skilled, did not have the courage to undertake anything attended just by an anesthetist and a nurse.

When she looked through the double glass door and saw the surgeon rush into the scrubbing-up room, she was relieved. He went straight to the sink, then dried his hands in the hot air from the hand dryer on the wall. He pulled on his gloves and headed for the operating theater. But instead of going in, he suddenly stopped in front of the door.

She stared at him in disbelief, not realizing why he was taking so long. And then it dawned on her what could be the reason. She hadn't worked with him yet, but she knew about the incident of the tweezers left inside a patient. Although he was reputed to be an excellent surgeon, this oversight had almost cost him his job.

The operation had taken place in this very room. He certainly must remember it in embarrassment whenever he went in. But now was not the time to let that memory get in his way. How could he fail to save the injured man whose life was hanging by a thread because of an incident that, however unpleasant, had nevertheless ended happily?

But the surgeon just stood there, staring straight ahead blankly, and she realized she had to break through the paralysis that bound him. The anesthetist and the nurse were clearly too disconcerted to do anything.

She waved at him to come in, but he didn't move. She called to him, but it was like talking to a deaf person. She finally went up to the door and called him in a louder voice. This didn't snap him out of it either.

She felt herself giving way to panic. Briskly opening the double door, she stretched out her hands towards his shoulders, wanting to shake him, but this wasn't necessary. He snapped out of it the moment she touched him.

She didn't remove her hands right away. They stayed there joined together for a few moments, gazing fixedly into each other's eyes. Had the circumstances been otherwise, one of them might have said something, but there was no time for idle chatter. They had to get straight to work.

Three hours and fourteen minutes later the patient was moved to the intensive care room. He had a long recovery ahead of him, but what counted was that he'd been brought back from the brink of death. The intern and surgeon never worked together again, so there was no chance to continue the conversation that they had never even started.

Translated from the Serbian by Alice Copple Tošić.

8

Infernal Library

The guard escorting me stopped before a door in the hallway and knocked. He waited for a few moments and then seemed to hear permission to enter, although nothing reached my ears. He opened the door, pushed me forward without a word, and stepped inside after me, grabbing hold of my shoulder to keep me there as he closed the door behind him. His grasp was unnecessarily firm since I had already stopped, not knowing what else to do. He probably didn't know how to be more gentle. We stood by the door, obviously awaiting new orders.

As with everything else I had seen so far, the ceiling was extremely high. This impression was accentuated here because the distance to the ceiling was considerably greater than the length and width of the room. I was suddenly overcome by the dizzying feeling that it would be more natural for the floor and one of the side walls to change places. But, of course, I could not expect the natural order of things to be maintained in this place. That time had passed for good. Who knew what unusual experiences

© Springer Nature Switzerland AG 2019
Z. Živković, *The Clay Writer*,
https://doi.org/10.1007/978-3-030-19753-7_8

were in store for me. I had to prepare myself for much worse.

The room was poorly lit and sparsely furnished. Hanging from the ceiling on a long wire, a weak bulb covered by a round metal shade shed most of its light on a backless wooden chair that stood by itself in the middle of the room. A man sat at a desk opposite the door, his back to the wall. Only visible above the shoulders, he concentrated on the computer screen in front of him. By the indistinct glow of the monitor, which created no shadow, his long face seemed almost ghostly pale. His short, thick beard appeared grizzled in the odd light and he wore semicircular reading glasses. I could not determine his age. He might have been anywhere from his early forties to his late fifties.

He didn't seem to notice us. The guard and I stood patiently by the door, as motionless as statues. Finally, without taking his eyes off the screen, the man raised his left hand and made a brief, vague gesture, which nonetheless had a clear meaning for the guard. He grabbed my shoulder roughly once again and led me towards the chair under the light. He released me only when I had sat down, then stood directly behind me.

While I waited, my gaze began to wander. The feeling of confinement caused by the height of the room was intensified by the uniformity of color around me. A sickly shade of olive-gray covered everything: the walls, the ceiling, the floor, the chair, the table. Even the monitor was olive-gray. The paint on the walls was cracked and peeling in places, showing patches of dry plaster the color of a stormy sky. It felt as if we were inside a faded and worn shoebox, once green, placed on end.

The room might have been less gloomy if there had been a window, even one with bars. But there were no windows. Working in a place like this could only be considered punishment. I looked at the person behind the monitor with a mixture of pity and dread. Even if I disregarded all the rest, there was certainly no reason to expect good of someone forced to work here for any period of time.

The deep silence in the room was suddenly broken by fingers tapping on a keyboard that I couldn't see. The rapid typing did not last long. When he was finished, the man raised his head, took off his glasses and laid them on the desk next to him. Then he squinted and pinched the bridge of his nose with his thumb and forefinger. He remained in this position for several moments before opening his eyes and nodding to the guard. The guard moved off at a brisk pace. The metal door opened with a squeak and then closed behind him.

We looked at each other without speaking for some time. I felt uncomfortable under his silent inspection, which expressed more aversion and bad temper than harshness or threat. I quickly realized that he wasn't the least bit happy about the upcoming conversation with me. He behaved like someone who has been doing the same job for too long to be able to find anything appealing in it. I had seen that expression on the faces of some older investigators and judges. Finally the man sighed, drew his fingers across his high forehead and broke the silence.

"You realize where you are, don't you?" He had a deep, drawling voice.

"In hell," I replied after hesitating a moment.

"That's right. Although we don't use that name anymore. Are you aware of why you have come to this place?"

I didn't answer right away. It was clear to me that there was no sense in hiding or denying anything, but I didn't exactly have to incriminate myself, either. "I can guess…"

"You can guess?" He raised his voice. "Even here we rarely see a dossier like this." He knocked the crook of his middle finger against the screen.

"I might be able to explain…"

"Don't!" he said, cutting me off. "Spare me, if you please! How inconsiderate you are, all of you who sit there. It isn't enough that I have to learn about the disgusting things you've done; you want me to listen to your phony, slime-ball explanations, too. They make me even sicker than the crimes themselves. In any case, there's nothing to explain. Everything is perfectly clear. We know all about you. Every detail. Would you be here if that weren't the case?"

"Mistakes do happen…" I noted softly.

"There are no mistakes," replied the man. "And even if there were, it's too late to rectify them. There's no way out of here. Once you're in, you stay for good."

I knew that, of course. Everyone knows that. But I still had to try.

"What about repentance? Does that mean anything?" I asked in the humblest of voices.

This time he didn't have to say anything. His expression told me exactly what he thought about my remorse.

"Don't waste your breath. I have no time for such non-sense. I'm inundated with work. The world has never been like this before. Can you imagine the burden on my shoulders?"

I could imagine, but since the question was rhetorical, I just shrugged. For a moment I thought the man wanted to complain to me about his hardships, but then he changed his mind.

"Forget it. It's not important. Let's get to the point. We have to find out what would suit you best."

"As punishment?" I asked cautiously.

"We call it therapy."

"Burning in fire is therapy?"

"Who's talking about burning in fire?"

"Maybe being boiled in oil or drawn and quartered…"

"Don't be vulgar! This isn't the Middle Ages!"

"Sorry, I didn't know…"

"It's simply unbelievable how many people come here with preconceived notions. Do you think we live outside the times? That nothing changes here? Would this go along with such barbaric brutality?" He tapped the side of the monitor.

"Of course not," I readily agreed.

"Every age has its own hell. Today it's a library."

I blinked in bewilderment. "A library?"

"Yes. A place where books are read. You have heard about libraries? Why is everyone so amazed when they find out?"

"It's a bit…unexpected."

"Only if you give it perfunctory consideration. Once you delve into the matter, you see that there's nothing unusual about it."

"It never would have crossed my mind."

"To tell you the truth, we were also a bit surprised at first. But what the computer told us was unequivocal. It is quite a useful machine."

He paused. Several moments passed before I understood what was expected of me. "Quite useful, indeed," I repeated.

"Particularly for statistical research. When we input data about everyone here, the trait that linked by far the greatest number of our inmates, 84.12% to be precise, was their aversion to reading. This was understandable for 26.38%, since they are completely illiterate. But what about the 47.71% who, although literate, had never picked up a single book, as though fearing the plague? The remaining ten or so percent read something here and there, but they'd wasted their time since it was totally worthless."

I nodded. "Who would have thought?"

He looked at me askance. "Why does that seem strange to you? Take yourself. How many books have you read?"

I thought it over briefly, trying to remember. "Well, er, not a whole lot, to tell the truth."

"Not a whole lot? I'll tell you exactly how many." The rapid sound of typing on the keyboard was heard once more. "In the past twenty-eight years of your life you started two books. You got halfway through the fourth page of the first, and in the second you didn't get beyond the introductory paragraph."

"It didn't catch my interest," I replied contritely.

"Really? And other things did?"

"I never suspected that not reading was a mortal sin."

"It isn't. Although the world would be a much better place if it were. No one's ever been sent to hell because they didn't read. That's why this trait was overlooked until we brought in the computer. But when, thanks to the computer, we noticed this connection, we were able to take advantage of it. In several ways. You might even say that it led to a true reform of hell."

"No one knows anything about that."

"Of course no one knows. How could anyone know? That's where all those prejudices come from. This place has never been the way most people imagine it: an eternal torture chamber run by merciless sadists. Tell me, do you smell that sulfur everyone talks about so much?"

I sniffed the air around me. It was dry and stale, a little musty. "No," I had to admit.

"We were simply a jail. With a few special features, that's true, but the system here differed very little from what you found in your jails. We treated our inmates here the same way you treated yours. Why should we be any different? If there was brutality and abuse here, that meant we were following your example. As conditions improved over time in your jails, the situation here became more bearable. Things went so far there was a danger of going against the basic idea of hell."

"What do you mean?"

"Recently your jails have almost been turned into recreation centers. You might even say they're modest hotels. You're the best judge of that; you spent a lot of time in jail, and it wasn't the least uncomfortable, right?"

I thought it over. "No, you're right, although the food wasn't always that good everywhere. Especially dessert."

A fleeting sigh escaped from the man behind the monitor. "There, you see. Well, now, we couldn't allow some of those privileges here. Weekend leaves, for instance. Or using cellular phones. How would that look?"

"But that would make it much easier to serve your time…"

"Perhaps. But it must never be forgotten that this is hell, after all. So we found ourselves in a bind. We couldn't follow the liberalization of conditions in your jails any longer. We were threatened with the one thing we have been accused of since time immemorial: being the incarnation of inhumanity and jeopardizing human rights. Luckily, that's when we found out about people not reading."

"Excuse me, but I don't see the connection."

"It was a simple matter. We made reading compulsory for everyone. This enabled us to combine the beautiful with the useful. First of all, our inmates could get rid of the main shortcoming that brought them here. If they had read more, they would have had less time and motive for misdeeds. Reading for them is truly healing. That is why we consider it therapy, not punishment, even though it might be a little late. But it is never really too late for something like that. And what do we call the place where everyone loves to read?"

"A library?"

The man spread his arms. "Of course. And a library is the last place to be accused of violating human rights, wouldn't you say? At the same time, this step removed the extremely embarrassing tarnish we had acquired. Furthermore, we turned out to be considerably more humane than your jails. They have libraries, of course, but what's the point, since they are almost never used? It's as though they don't even exist. Take your own case once again. Did you ever go into a library in one of the many jails you were in?"

"I didn't even know they had them," I replied truthfully.

"What did I tell you? But don't worry, you'll soon have a chance to make up for what you've missed. And much more than that, in effect. Before you is literally a whole eternity of reading."

I stared at the man for several moments without speaking. "So that's my punishment? Reading?"

"Therapy."

"Therapy, yes. There won't be anything else?" I tried to suppress the sound of relief in my voice, but without success.

"Nothing else, of course. You will sit in your cell and read. That's all. You won't have any other obligation. I must, however, draw your attention to the fact that eternity is a very long time. You might get bored with reading at some point. That happens to many of our inmates and then they become very clever. My, what tricks they resort to, giving the impression that they're reading, even though they aren't. But we have ways to see through all those crafty ploys. In such cases we must, unfortunately, use forceful means to get them to return to reading. With the most resistant and stubborn they are sometimes rather painful, I'm afraid."

"What about human rights? Humanity?"

"We don't lay a hand on them. This is exclusively for their own good. We can't let them harm themselves out of spiritual indolence, can we?"

"I suppose not," I replied, not quite convinced.

"Those are the main things you should know. You will grow accustomed to conditions here. It will probably be a little difficult at first, until you get used to it, but you will finally realize that reading offers incomparable satisfaction. Everyone becomes aware of this during eternity, some sooner and some later. I hope in the meantime that you behave in a mature and sober manner and do not compel us to resort to force. That will make it nice and easy for everyone."

Since my unquestioning agreement was clearly understood, I nodded. For the first time, the corners of the man's mouth turned up a little, forming the shadow of a smile.

"Fine. Now let's see which therapy would suit you best. What kind of reading material would you prefer?"

It was a difficult question, so I took my time answering it. "Maybe detective stories," I said finally, in a half-questioning tone.

"Ah, certainly not!" replied the man, frowning again. "That would be like giving a sick man poison instead of medicine. No, you need something quite the opposite. Something mild, gentle, enriching. Pastoral works, for example. Yes, that is the right choice for your soul. Idylls. We often prescribe them. They have a truly wondrous effect."

He saw an expression on my face that might have been disgust. When he spoke again his voice had returned to its initial sharpness.

"If you think this unjust, you can take consolation in the fact that I would give anything to be in your shoes. Enjoying idylls. At least for a while. But I can't, unfortunately. They won't let me. Instead, I am forced to read exclusively the abominations and baseness that simply gush out of here. Like water from a broken dam." He tapped the monitor again, this time on top. "And eternity for me is no shorter than it is for you. That's not fair. Whenever you hit crisis-point, just think how much I envy you, and you'll feel better."

He stopped talking. The incongruous height and dreary color of the room suddenly seemed to collapse in on him, twisting his face into a mask of contempt and despair. He looked at me a moment longer, his eyes turning blank. Before he reached for his glasses and put them on again, he turned his head towards the door behind me. He didn't say a word, but it squeaked right away. The guard's firm hand found my shoulder. I got up off the chair under the light bulb and headed outside. On the way, I took another look at the man behind the desk. He had almost completely sunk behind the monitor, engrossed in a new dossier. A moment later the door hid him from my view, and I set off down the hall with the guard towards my cell, where an eternity of reading awaited me as well.

Translated from the Serbian by Alice Copple Tošić.

9

Annotations 2

Six pieces of my fiction, used as models for various topics I assigned to my students, had originally been written during a period of fifteen years, 1993–2008. Here they are in chronological order: "Sherlock Holmes' Last Case: The Letter" (in *The Fourth Circle*, a novel, 1993), "Infernal Library" (in *The Library*, a mosaic novel, 2002), "The Telephone" (a stand-alone story, 2004), " Fingernails" (in *Twelve Collections*, a mosaic novel, 2005), "Lost Illusions" (in *Amarcord*, a mosaic novel, 2007) and "The First Loop" (in *Escher's Loops*, a novel, 2008).

Three of these six pieces are segments of my mosaic novels and two are chapters from two separate novels. Regardless of their being part of a larger narrative whole, they can be read as stand-alone stories. The last of them, "The First Loop", was written just in time to be used in my first academic year, 2007–2008. In fact, on that first occasion I read it in manuscript, since the book was not yet published.

© Springer Nature Switzerland AG 2019
Z. Živković, *The Clay Writer*,
https://doi.org/10.1007/978-3-030-19753-7_9

While reading stories to my students, I often tested both how insightful they were as readers (listeners, in fact) and how predictable I was as a writer. I broke off the reading occasionally in order to ask them to try and guess what followed next in a story or how it ended. They were seldom successful. Of course, had they been more diligent, they could have read my stories in advance, since it was no secret which ones I had chosen for my course, but they never took pains to do extra reading. So as to avoid unnecessary disappointment, I never asked them whether they had been inspired by what they had heard in class to read the rest of the larger whole to which a story belonged…

Regardless of this uncertainty, it was a tradition that I give each of my students a book of mine as a New Year gift at the very end of the first semester. We also took a group photo on that occasion which I subsequently posted on my official website. Images of all ten generations of my creative writing students are still there.

Once I got in return two small, symbolic presents from them. They referred to the first two themes we had worked on in the first semester: a conversation between the writer and the devil and a pastiche of Sherlock Holmes. My students insisted that I apply them right away. Although reluctantly, I had no alternative but to agree—to their great amusement. Needless to say, I was immortalized by as many mobile phone cameras as there were around. One of these numerous photos is still on my website too. It is also exclusively included in this edition of *The Clay Writer* (page 58). For better or worse…